One kiss from those lips . . .

would never be enough. If he took even a single step closer, it would be too late to turn back.

The electricity that sizzled between them was so strong, so compelling that both were being burned by it. She didn't want this. Smoldering passion terrified her. She'd put aside those needs long ago and learned to channel her energy into a drive that she could control—the drive to succeed.

"If you'll excuse me, Mr. Andrews, I have an employee waiting in my office."

"This isn't over, Miss Porter."

She blinked. She'd hoped this little incident could be put aside. "Oh, but it is. And I'm sure you'll be gentleman enough to keep your distance."

"Don't bet on it."

Dear Reader,

Welcome to Silhouette. Experience the magic of the wonderful world where two people fall in love. Meet heroines who will make you cheer for their happiness, and heroes (be they the boy next door or a handsome, mysterious stranger) who will win your heart. Silhouette Romances reflect the magic of love—sweeping you away with books that will make you laugh and cry, heartwarming, poignant stories that will move you time and time again.

In the next few months, we're publishing romances by many of your all-time favorites, such as Diana Palmer, Brittany Young, Emilie Richards and Arlene James. Your response to these authors and other authors of Silhouette Romances has served as a touchstone for us, and we're pleased to bring you more books with Silhouette's distinctive medley of charm, wit and—above all—*romance*.

I hope you enjoy this book and the many stories to come. Experience the magic!

Sincerely,

Tara Hughes
Senior Editor
Silhouette Books

RUTH LANGAN
The Proper Miss Porter

Silhouette Romance

Published by Silhouette Books New York
America's Publisher of Contemporary Romance

To Mike
Artist, Dreamer, Architect

SILHOUETTE BOOKS
300 E. 42nd St., New York, N.Y. 10017

ISBN: 0-373-08492-7

First Silhouette Books printing March 1987

Books by Ruth Langan

Silhouette Romance

Just Like Yesterday #121
Hidden Isle #224
No Gentle Love #303
Eden of Temptation #317
This Time Forever #371
Family Secrets #407
Mysteries of the Heart #458
The Proper Miss Porter #492

Silhouette Special Edition

Beloved Gambler #119
To Love a Dreamer #218
Star-Crossed #266
Whims of Fate #354

RUTH LANGAN

enjoys writing about modern men and women who are not afraid to be both strong and tender. Her sense of humor is evident in her work. Happily married to her childhood sweetheart, she thrives on the chaos created by two careers and five children.

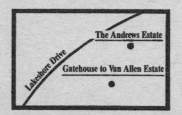

The Andrews Estate

Lakeshore Drive

Gatehouse to Van Allen Estate

LAKE SUPERIOR

ONTARIO, CANADA

WISCONSIN

LAKE MICHIGAN

Torch Lake

Van Allen Cottage

LAKE HURON

Grand Rapids

Lansing

Pontiac

Detroit

MICHIGAN
Underlined places are fictitious.

LAKE ERIE

INDIANA

OHIO

Chapter One

Here are the two personnel files you requested." Martha James paused beside the enormous slab of rosewood that served as her boss's desk. "I take it one of these will be the new manager of Division Two?"

Gray eyes slowly appraised her. If she hadn't been secretary to his father for twenty years before Clif Andrews assumed the presidency of Andrews Motors, she would have wilted beneath that icy stare. He was well aware that all his other employees did. But she had known him when he was an awkward teen. That, and the fact that he had urged her to stay on after his father's death, gave her a certain amount of self-assurance.

Ignoring her impertinence, he asked, "Has everyone been notified of the meeting this afternoon?"

"All but your aunt. Her housekeeper said she won't be back from LaCosta until tomorrow."

"Marion's vote is only necessary to break a tie. I'm sure the board will accept my decision as final." While Clif spoke, he picked up the first manila folder and sorted through the contents.

"Bill Campbell's a good man," Martha said, noting the glossy photo. "Top of his class at Ohio State. Worked his tail off at the Tech Center."

Spreading the contents of the second folder on the opposite side of his desk, Clif lifted out the photo.

"Alexandra Porter's his equal," Martha went on a little too enthusiastically.

She avoided Clif's eyes when he slanted a look at her.

"Worked her way through Michigan State. Did every job the company handed her. When Martin took that leave of absence, she practically ran the engine-testing division single-handedly."

"That so? Martha, you wouldn't be trying to influence my decision, would you?"

She gave a self-conscious grin. "Just wanted you to take your time. These promotions don't come up every day."

He was only too aware of that fact. Hadn't he started at the very bottom after college? Some of the jobs he'd held had been sheer drudgery. He had served in almost every department of the family company, determined to prove himself. He had been the youngest vice president of Andrews Motors at the time of his father's untimely death. Despite his youth, the board of directors had rewarded his diligence by unanimously electing him president.

Glancing at his watch, he said, "Hold all my phone calls for the next hour. I want to study these files one more time."

The hour stretched into two, making it impossible for Clif to eat lunch before the board meeting. He closed both files and rubbed a weary hand over his eyes. The candidates were equally qualified. Both had fine academic records. Both had demonstrated a willingness to work hard. Both had been called on to make difficult decisions, which later had turned out to be the right ones. But one candidate had something extra. Despite the pressures of being young and female, Alexandra Porter had earned the respect of the other employees, not only her peers in midlevel management, but the people on the line. That made her invaluable.

"Alexandra." Only once had an employee tried to shorten her name to Alex. Her ensuing lecture, delivered in that quiet tone everyone respected, left no doubt about her feelings on the matter.

"Alexandra." Mike Miller's booming voice could shake buildings. "Call on line one. Top brass."

Alexandra lifted the phone, wondering for the hundredth time this day if it could be the call she'd been praying for.

"Alexandra Porter here."

"Miss Porter." The woman's voice was high-pitched with excitement. "I'm Mr. Andrews's secretary. This is to notify you that your name is being offered to the board for the position of manager of Division Two. The board will have to ratify the nomination at one o'clock. Mr. Andrews asks that you present yourself at the boardroom at one-thirty. As you know, he believes in personally introducing new managers to the board."

Alexandra couldn't think of a single thing to say.

"Congratulations, Miss Porter. You've certainly earned this promotion."

"Thank you, Miss..."

"James. Martha James."

"Thank you, Miss James. I'll be there at one-thirty."

As she replaced the receiver, she looked up to see Mike lounging in the doorway. His curly blond hair, blue eyes and weight-lifter's physique made him the darling of the secretarial pool. He'd been her assistant for two years. Though she'd never said a word about wanting this promotion, she was certain Mike had sensed her uneasiness these past weeks.

"Anything I should know?"

In a breathless voice she whispered, "I'm to be the new manager of Division Two."

His eyes lit with real pleasure. "This isn't a put-on?"

She shook her head, too overwhelmed to speak.

"All right!" He let out a whoop and swung her around, then, sensing her embarrassment at his outburst, he set her on her feet and offered his hand. "Congratulations, Ms. Manager."

"Thank you. Oh, Mike." She covered her face with her hands, afraid for a moment that she might break down and cry. Then, lifting her chin, she sniffed and squared her shoulders. "I can't believe it."

"You'll believe it when you see that first fat paycheck."

"I'm going to celebrate."

"Atta girl. Break out the champagne."

Her cool look dampened his enthusiasm. "Did you say you had two extra tickets to the Wolverine game Sunday?"

At his nod, she said, "I'll buy them from you."

He gave her a quizzical look. "I didn't know you liked football."

"I usually can't spare the time." She shrugged. "But . . . someone I know loves the game."

Someone she knew? The tone of her voice told him it was someone special. Mike knew better than to pry. Alexandra Porter was the most private woman he'd ever met. After working alongside her for two years, he still knew nothing about her life away from the office. Invariably, she politely refused to join the others on their regular Friday evening stopover at a nearby singles' bar.

He gave her a flashing smile. "Better yet, I'll give them to you. My gift to the new manager of Division Two."

"Oh, Mike, that's sweet. Thank you." She seemed flustered. "Now, if you'll excuse me, I have some important calls to make."

She turned away, striving for the composure she'd always been able to display in times of excitement or stress.

Alexandra halted for a moment in the doorway. This was her first glimpse of the boardroom. The walls were paneled in rich, warm mahogany. A portrait of the firm's founder, Cyrus Quin Andrews, was hung in a place of honor. Slightly below it hung the portrait of his son, Cyril Quin Andrews, the current president's father. A carpet bearing the firm's logo seemed to stretch on endlessly. A conference table dominated the room. Nine chairs were placed on either side of it, with two more at either end. At each place was a leather-bound notebook and an ebony pen, as well as a crystal tumbler. Pitchers of ice water were placed within reach around the table.

There was only one vacant chair. At least, Alexandra thought, she wouldn't have to ask where to sit. Her chair was at the opposite end of the table from the president. When she glanced up, she realized everyone in the room was staring at her. Even the president.

Clif's gaze was arrested by the mass of auburn curls twisted into a knot on top of Alexandra Porter's proudly tilted head. The black-and-white glossy photograph hadn't prepared him for this lush redhead. Her eyes were the most intense shade of green he'd ever seen. Her skin was pale, her complexion flawless. Not a single freckle marred her flushed cheeks, her tiny upturned nose.

"Congratulations, Ms. Porter. May I present our board of directors."

As Clif spoke each name, he continued studying the young woman before him.

Her charcoal suit was perfectly tailored to fit her slender frame. Yet soft womanly curves were evident. The prim white blouse she wore was brightened by a silk foulard tie in shades of blue and green, enhancing her vivid coloring.

Realizing he was staring, he cleared his throat. "The only absent member of the board is my aunt, Marion Andrews. I'm certain she would add her voice to mine in welcoming you to our management family."

"Thank you, Mr. Andrews."

He hadn't been expecting that voice. Low and smoky like a blues singer's, it touched something deep inside him.

With an effort, he tore his gaze away to encompass the entire assembly. "And now, I'll accept a motion for adjournment. That way, the members can offer you their individual good wishes."

Feeling overwhelmed by the handshakes and congratulations that followed, Alexandra stood stiffly, murmuring appropriate responses.

Clif paused at the door. He'd intended to leave quickly. The work on his desk was never-ending. Still he hesitated, enjoying the scene. To prolong his stay, he turned back and spoke to one of the board members. While the voice beside him droned on, he listened for the sound of Miss Porter's low, almost husky tones. The group began moving toward the door. When she stepped beside him, he held out his hand, forcing her to stop.

"Congratulations again, Miss Porter."

Her head barely reached his shoulder. He'd had no idea she was so small. He saw the way her eyebrow arched as their fingers touched. Cool. Her hand was cool; her handshake firm.

Alexandra had seen Clif Andrews hundreds of times during the years she'd worked for the company. She recalled that when she'd worked in the engineering department, he had dropped by almost daily to study the new prototypes. He'd never noticed her; he saw nothing except the cars. It was obvious that he was in love with the automobile. It was his passion.

As always, his dark suit was impeccable, carefully tailored to mold his wide shoulders and narrow waist and hips. His thick black hair was razor short. She could read nothing in his slate-gray eyes. Behind his back the employees of Andrews Motors called him "the Ice Man." It suited him. He held himself aloof from his employees. He prowled about the various departments, poking, prodding, familiarizing himself with every detail of his cars' assembly, without ever getting to know the people who turned out the product.

Very firmly she withdrew her hand. "Thank you, Mr. Andrews."

There was nothing else to say. She moved through the doorway and was gone. Behind her lingered the heady fragrance of an autumn woods.

Clif hesitated for a moment longer. Why did the fragrance of Alexandra Porter seem so at odds with her prim, businesslike appearance? And why should that bother him so? He pulled open the door with more force than necessary. When he passed his secretary, she was puzzled by the grim line of his mouth.

"Just a moment, Mr. Andrews."

Martha handed her boss a sheaf of papers as he strolled toward the door. Snapping open his briefcase, he stuffed them inside. As usual, Clif's briefcase was bulging with work he'd have to do over the weekend.

Outside the door to the executive offices, a limousine purred in the frosty air. The uniformed driver opened the door, then closed it as Clif slid inside.

By the time the vehicle passed through the gates, Clif's head was bent over his paperwork. Long ago, he'd had to give up the luxury of driving himself to and from work. These were precious hours he could devote to work unfinished at the office.

As the limousine passed Alexandra's car, she studied the tinted windows that made the occupants invisible. She knew it was the president's car. Everyone in the company was familiar with it. It was one more symbol of his wealth and power. One more way to set himself apart from his employees.

At the intersection she turned left and entered the expressway with hundreds of other commuters. She snapped on the radio and winced at the blare of pop music. Twisting the dial, she found her favorite station. With the haunting wail of a tenor sax playing in the background, she slowly changed mental gears, allowing the pressures of work to slip away before facing the very different role she played at home.

Sighing, she brushed back an errant wisp of hair and tried, unsuccessfully, to forget about Clif Andrews. She shivered, for the second time that day. She hadn't expected to feel anything when the president of the company shook her hand. But even now, hours later, she could recall the tingling sensation that simple touch had caused. She brought a hand to her warm cheek. Too hot. Kid stuff. She thought she'd put all this behind her. She would not allow a man, and an arrogant one at that, to occupy her mind. It was the excitement of the promotion, she assured herself. Though she'd kept her emotions under control at the board meeting, it meant everything to her to become manager of Division Two. Her own department. This made up for the long hours, the missed weekends. This justified the years of working her way through college and missing entire nights of sleep, cramming for finals and juggling two lives. She'd show them. She'd show all of them.

Alexandra turned the car into the driveway of a turreted stone gatehouse. It had once been the caretaker's cottage of a waterfront estate. Years ago the mansion had been leveled and the property developed into a posh subdivision. Now all that remained of that elegant estate was this building. Though the houses around it were more luxurious, they lacked its classic design.

Switching off the engine, she hurried up the walk, slinging her purse over her shoulder as she went.

The door was pulled open even before she reached it.

"You're late. You've got to talk to her. She must have inherited that obstinate streak from you."

Alexandra stared at the woman whose enormous bulk filled the doorway. Milly Bingham lived three doors away. When her husband had died several years earlier, she'd considered going back to the work force she'd left thirty years before. But seeing Alexandra's need for a housekeeper, she'd simply taken over and made herself indispensable.

The purple floral dress she wore drifted nearly to her ankles. The neck was tied with fuzzy pom-poms. On her feet were faded purple scuffs. Purple was her favorite color this month. But it was her hair that held Alexandra's fascinated gaze. Bright red-orange, it stuck out in little tufts around her face. Yesterday it had been shoulder length and jet-black.

Seeing the direction of Alexandra's gaze, Milly smiled. "Like it?"

"It's—umm—interesting."

"I found an old photo of Fontayne in a red wig. I know I can improve my exercises with this color."

"I see." Strangely enough, she did. Alexandra understood that the woman inside Milly was a ballerina. Despite her size and age, despite the difficulty she experienced at the barre, she was, in her mind, a dancer. It wasn't at all unusual to find her pausing in her work to bend her knees and dip gracefully, back erect, head high, in a *grand plié*.

Alexandra had to wait until her housekeeper moved aside before she could pass. "Now what's Charley being obstinate about?"

"Humm? Oh, she won't let me wash her hair in olive oil."

"Why would you want to do that, Milly?"

"Millicent."

Alexandra gave her a quizzical look.

"I said 'Millicent.' It's so much more elegant than Milly, don't you think?"

Alexandra nodded, knowing her housekeeper would sort through the confusion in her own way.

"Charley was complaining about static electricity when she brushed her hair. I assured her olive oil would take care of the problem."

"Maybe she doesn't want to smell like a salad. A humidifier would be simpler. Where is she?"

"Upstairs, keeping out of my way. Congratulations."

As always, Alexandra kept up with the erratic twists in the conversation. "Thanks."

"I couldn't believe it when you called. You never even gave a hint that you were in line for a promotion."

Alexandra's green eyes danced with excitement. "Oh, Milly...Millicent. I was afraid it would be bad luck to talk about it."

"I made something special to celebrate. Roast beef and all the trimmings."

Tossing her purse on the sofa, Alexandra inhaled. "Smells wonderful. You'll stay for dinner?" She didn't really need to ask. It was simply a formality. Milly loved to eat almost as much as she loved to cook.

As Alexandra started toward the stairs, Milly called, "Tell Charley 'impotent.'"

Alexandra paused. Turning, she arched an eyebrow.

"She needed an eight-letter word meaning 'lacking in power or vigor.' I just thought of it. Impotent."

A grin curled the corners of Alexandra's lips. "Thanks, I'll tell her."

"She spends too much time with those puzzles. I've never seen anyone as fascinated with words as that girl."

"Comes from all those books she read to amuse herself while I studied."

Hurrying up the stairs, Alexandra stood in the doorway for a moment, staring at the figure sprawled across the bed. A mass of fiery tangles spilled forward, obscuring the girl's face. A pair of faded boy's chinos and a khaki shirt had become her favorite uniform. They hung loosely on her thin frame. She was small for her eight years, just as Alexandra had been. And into her tomboy stage.

"Hi, Charley. Milly says 'impotent.' "

Charley's green eyes widened slightly. Her head tilted. "Millicent. She's not answering to 'Milly' today."

"I forgot."

"I already figured out the word." Deliberately she dropped her pencil before leaping from the bed and hurling herself into Alexandra's arms.

"You did it. Mom, you did it."

"You've got to thump it. Like this." Charley bent over the pumpkin, flicking her finger against the thick outer layer.

Row after endless row of pumpkins lay scattered in the field. Now that the corn had been harvested, the bright orange mounds were clearly visible for acres. As Charley walked slowly between the rows, her tousled hair was only a few shades darker than the pumpkins.

Pressing her ear closer, she said, "Listen, Mom. This one sounds full."

"I can't imagine what difference that makes. We're going to scrape out the insides before we carve the face, anyway."

"I told you. I found an article in the paper about drying the pumpkin seeds and baking them in the oven. And Milly promised to bake a pumpkin pie if you save her all the junky insides."

"Pulp. It sounds better than 'junky insides.'"

"Yeah. Pulp. So we want a big fat full pumpkin. I say this is the one."

Like a pro, Charley turned it over and carefully examined all sides for bruises. Her Halloween pumpkin had to be perfect. Satisfied, she struggled to separate it from the vine. Tugging with all her might, she went sprawling backward in the dirt when it suddenly gave way.

Mother and daughter giggled. Standing up, Charley dusted off the seat of her pants and lifted the pumpkin. It was nearly as big as she.

"Can I take it to be weighed?"

"It might be better if you let it take you."

"I'm stronger than I look. See?"

Bobbing and weaving under the weight, she stumbled toward the scales at the fruit stand.

"I'll meet you up there," Alexandra called to her retreating back. "I'm going to pick a bouquet of mums."

From the time Charley was born, Alexandra had thrown herself into shared weekend activities with a vengeance. She knew she was trying to ease her guilt at having to be away from her daughter during the long workweek. But though she often found herself doing things she'd never dreamed of trying, she would have been the first to admit she cherished these hours.

The afternoon sun had burned off the frost but hadn't eliminated the chill in the air. Drawing the lapels of her suede jacket together, she casually flung one end of her scarf over her shoulder as she bent to pick the flowers.

* * *

The limousine idled in the weed-strewn section of the farm reserved for parking. While the uniformed driver waited inside with the heater humming, Clif leaned against the rear fender, his arms crossed over his chest. On the way from the airport, Marion had insisted on stopping for fresh fruit and flowers. He watched her haggle with one of the young workers. Turning his attention to the fields, he stiffened suddenly.

In a sea of pumpkins, a slender figure straightened. There was only one woman he knew with hair that color. Straining, he watched as she flung her scarf over her shoulder, making a slash of white against the brown jacket.

"Are you just going to stand there, or are you going to open the door?" Marion couldn't hide the impatience in her voice.

"Oh, sorry." He opened the door for his aunt, closed it after her, then paused to watch as the figure walked closer.

Orange, yellow, purple and white mums filled her arms. Even brilliant blooms couldn't compete with her beauty.

The driver opened his door. "Is there something you want, Mr. Andrews?"

Clif's lips lifted in a smile. "Umm. You might say that."

Rounding the car, he settled himself inside. As the vehicle pulled away, he turned. She was close enough for him to see her dazzling smile as a sudden breeze caught the ends of her hair, whipping them across her cheeks. Then the limousine sped off.

When Alexandra arrived at the stand, Charley had already had the pumpkin weighed.

"Vernon says I probably got the best pumpkin in the whole patch."

"Vernon?"

"Charley and I didn't take long to know each other. By now we feel like old friends." The elderly farmer looked up from his scale to give her a smile. "Charley told me you're going to dry the seeds." He chuckled. "We compared recipes."

"And he says mine's better."

Alexandra smiled indulgently. Holding out the bouquet, she said, "Add these to our bill. What do we owe you, Mr.... Vernon?"

"Eight dollars and fifty cents." He counted out her change from a ten-dollar bill.

"Vernon says I look like I sprang up from a pumpkin patch."

The old man laughed. "With that red hair, I couldn't tell her from the rest of my garden."

"But I told him I belong to you. And you know what he said?"

Alexandra shook her head. It was so like her daughter. Everywhere they went, Charley managed to make a friend, and usually managed to know his or her business before she left. Of course, along the way, she managed to tell a great deal about herself and her mother, as well.

"He said you were just about the prettiest pumpkin he'd ever seen."

At Alexandra's slight flush, the farmer chuckled. "I told Charley I'd like to hire both of you every autumn to stand in my garden and attract customers."

"But I told him you already have a good job at Andrews Motors. And now that you're manager of your own division, you won't have time to sell pumpkins. Even though it'd be fun," she added wistfully.

The farmer lifted the pumpkin. "Where's your car?"

With Charley running ahead with the trunk key, the farmer and Alexandra followed more slowly.

"You have a sweet little girl, ma'am," he said. "She just makes a body happy to be around her."

"Thank you. I'm always afraid her chattering will bother strangers."

He gave a derisive snort. "With all the troubles in the world, it's nice to see someone friendly and unspoiled. I got a real kick out of talking to her."

Setting the pumpkin in the trunk, the farmer closed the lid and handed the key to Alexandra. Turning to Charley, he winked. "My offer stands. Anytime you want to sell pumpkins, you just let me know."

"Thanks, Vernon." Very formally she accepted his handshake, then climbed into the car.

As they drove away, Charley turned to watch the maze of orange on the hillside until it disappeared in the distance.

"He was a nice man, Mom. Told me to sprinkle a little salt on the pumpkin seeds before baking them."

"That's a good thing to remember." Alexandra waited a moment, unsure how to proceed. She cleared her throat. "Charley. I'm proud of the fact that you make friends so easily. But . . . I don't think you should tell strangers about our personal affairs."

"Like what?" With her index finger she drew round faces on the foggy window. All of them had smiles.

"Like my job. My new promotion."

"Vernon thought that was terrific. He said you looked too young to be a manager."

"He was just being polite."

The little girl turned slowly. In that brief instant, Alexandra had a glimpse of the knowledgeable woman hidden inside the child. "Mom, don't you think you look young and pretty?"

Alexandra looked away, keeping her eyes on the road.

"I mean," the little girl persisted, "even when you tie your hair back in that dumb bun and wear those men's suits, don't you notice how men look at you sometimes?'' Her tone was wistful. ''Billy Peters says you're prettier than any movie star.''

''Does Billy Peters need glasses?''

''He thinks I'm pretty, too.''

''Brilliant. The boy is absolutely brilliant. And he has very good taste. I like that boy already.''

Alexandra was relieved at her daughter's childish laughter. Glancing at her watch, she muttered, ''We've got to hustle. The Wolverine game starts at two o'clock.''

''I still can't believe we're going. You're going to love it, Mom.''

While Charley fiddled with the radio dial, Alexandra fell silent. Sometime, sometime when she had it all prepared, she'd have a talk with Charley. Careless chatter, like idle gossip, could cause pain. An innocent remark could cause people to turn away from her. She had to be warned that people could be cruel. Alexandra lifted her sunglasses to the top of her head. But not today. Not yet. She'd buy a little more time. Charley deserved the right to childish trust for as long as possible.

''Let's not eat at home, Mom. Let's eat at the stadium.''

''Are you sure? There's probably nothing but half-cooked hot dogs.''

''Where's your sense of adventure?''

Alexandra turned her head. Two pairs of green eyes met, then glowed with laughter.

''Oh. So you think I'm too...careful, do you?'' She swung the car into the driveway and unfastened her seat belt with a dramatic flair. ''Watch out, world. Two pumpkin heads are about to set out on an adventure.''

Giggling like two conspirators, they hauled their purchases into the house, then hurried upstairs to change.

Chapter Two

"Got the tickets?"

"Right here." Alexandra patted her purse.

"Know where we're sitting?"

"I guess we'll just follow these arrows to our section. If we get lost, I'll ask someone. Want some peanuts?"

Charley bought two bags and stuck the change in the back pocket of her jeans. All around them vendors hawked shirts and hats, souvenirs, programs. Like a teeming ant colony, swarms of people continued to pour through the doors of the stadium. It seemed impossible that any structure could hold so many bodies. Despite the surge of the crowd, Alexandra was surprised at the orderliness of the procession.

"Do you suppose they all know where they're going?" Alexandra asked.

Charley shrugged. "Come on. I see our section up here."

Racing ahead, she read the numbers on the rows and flew back to her mother's side.

"I thought double A would be back here somewhere. But these are all single letters. Do you know what that means?"

Unimpressed, Alexandra shook her head.

"Mom. It means we're in the front row. We're practically on the field. Come on." Tugging on Alexandra's sleeve, Charley hustled her toward their seats.

"Mike told me they were good seats. I never dreamed they'd be this good." Alexandra bent and carefully dusted the seat with her program. Beside her, two men drinking beer admired the view.

"Oh. Let's get a hot dog," Charley called as a vendor made his way through the stands.

Waving her hand, Alexandra caught his attention.

After the first bite, she rolled her eyes heavenward. "I'd forgotten how good a hot dog could taste at a game."

With a deafening roar from the crowd, the two teams charged onto the field. By kickoff time she and Charley had managed to polish off the hot dogs and peanuts and had washed them down with two large grape sodas.

Clif instructed the attendants where to set up the cocktails and hors d'oeuvres in his private box at the stadium. Years ago, his father had begun the custom of taking a box to entertain executives of the company as well as important clients and friends. Though he considered these brief hours at the stadium his only real time to relax, Clif was reluctant to discontinue the tradition. There were competitors in the business who would be all too happy to compare him unfavorably with his predecessors. Besides, as owner of the Wolverine team, he was expected to entertain at all home games.

As the guests began arriving, he noted his aunt singling out the daughter of one of their biggest shareholders. Groaning inwardly, he steeled himself. From the time he was in college, she'd been determined that he "make a good match."

"Clif, you remember Marguerite Van Horn?"

Swathed in silver fox the exact shade of her platinum hair, the woman gave him an approving look.

He extended his hand. "Miss Van Horn."

"Marguerite." When he broke contact, she dropped her hand to his sleeve.

Marion hovered nearby with a satisfied smile.

"It was so good of you to invite my father and me," Marguerite purred. "We'd like to reciprocate by taking you to dinner at the club later."

Cool metallic-looking eyes met hers. "Sorry. I'm afraid I've already made other plans." He had an intimidating way of staring a person down.

She felt a chill along her spine. "Couldn't we persuade you to change them?"

"Not possible. But thank you."

He turned away to greet a cluster of guests who were helping themselves to the appetizers.

Behind him, the young woman continued to stare. There was something aloof, something almost arrogant about Clif Andrews. He wore the finest clothes, and wore them with style. He lived in one of the most elegant mansions on Lakeshore Drive. Everyone knew he'd inherited one of the most successful auto companies in the country. If he chose, he wouldn't have to work another day. At every charity function he was photographed with a beautiful woman on his arm. He'd dated and discarded so many she'd need a scorecard to keep track of them all. Yet no woman had been able to hold his interest for very long. As he bent to whisper to his aunt, Marguerite continued to watch, fascinated. She wouldn't be discouraged. She wasn't just any woman. She'd simply bide her time and wait for the next opportunity.

"Tony." Clif flashed one of his rare smiles and clasped a tall, bearded man in a bear hug. The two had been childhood friends. When they'd elected to attend rival colleges, a good-natured wager on the two schools' football teams had grown into an annual event. Even though Tony was now a corporate lawyer in New York, they managed to maintain their friendship. "I was beginning to think you wouldn't make it."

"You mean you were hoping I wouldn't," Tony said with a laugh. "This is the first time in three years that my college team beat yours. I wouldn't miss this for anything."

"You're determined to get your revenge, aren't you?" Despite his sarcastic tone, Clif's face was wreathed in smiles.

"Damned right. Especially after last year's humiliation." His voice lowered. "Do you know what it felt like to wear clown makeup and ride an oversize tricycle in Macy's Thanksgiving Day Parade?"

With a straight face, Clif said, "I thought you were the best clown in the parade."

"If anyone had recognized me . . ."

"How could they? Besides, a bet is a bet."

"Right you are, buddy. And now that the shoe is on the other foot, it's going to be sweet." Tony glanced around. "Ready?"

Clif gave a grudging nod and bent to whisper to his aunt. "I have to leave for a little while, Marion. I'm sure you can entertain our guests."

"Clif." His aunt caught his arm. "Where are you going? The game is going to start any minute now."

He gave her an indulgent smile. "I'll probably have to miss the first half. But I'll be back in plenty of time to visit with everyone after the game."

With his old friend beside him, Clif began weaving through the cluster of guests, pausing to chat so that his exit would be as inconspicuous as possible. Finally he made his way quickly out the door. Behind him, the beautiful blonde felt a stab of disappointment. He hadn't even glanced her way.

When Clif and Tony reached the team locker room, it was empty except for an elderly attendant who shuffled about neatly stacking towels. He gave Clif a toothless smile, then disappeared into the showers.

Looking around like a thief, Tony knocked on the office door. It was opened a crack by a thin young man. After a quick glance, he opened the door wide enough to permit them to enter.

"Do you have it?" Tony asked.

The young man nodded and pointed to the furry costume draped across the desk.

"If you'll let me off the hook, I'll make a sizable contribution to your favorite charity," Clif offered.

Tony held up a hand. "No chance. You lost the bet; you pay the consequences."

Turning to the younger man, Clif said brusquely, "Not a word of this to anyone. If there's even a hint, I'll have your job."

The young man nodded his assent, then lifted the furry costume and held it out to Clif.

Quickly removing his suit jacket and tie, Clif stepped into the one-piece garment and zipped it closed. As he pulled on the head covering and half mask, he heard chuckles and whirled. "All right, you two," he said through gritted teeth, "have your laughs in here. But if you tell a soul..."

"Stop complaining and get on with it. The terms of the bet were that you would spend the entire first half of the game posing as your team mascot. Here," Tony said, handing Clif an assortment of makeup. "Finish your face."

The two men watched as Clif drew whiskers and a bright red mouth.

Wiping away tears of laughter, Tony chuckled and said, "You get better looking every minute. Go out there and charm the fans."

With a last glance in the mirror, Clif groaned at his reflection. Squaring his shoulders, he walked out, completely transformed.

While the team called a time-out, the announcer in the booth said in an excited voice, "The cheering you hear in the background is for our mascot, Wooly the Wolverine. Just listen to that crowd respond."

The fans on their side of the stadium let out a roar, and Alexandra and Charley craned their necks to see what was causing the disturbance. Running onto the field was a man in a wolverine costume, complete with dark brown fur with lighter brown bands on either side and a wonderful half mask of fur around his upper face. Beneath the whiskers, the mouth had been painted into a brilliant smile.

"It's Wooly," Charley screeched above the din. "Mom, look. Wooly the Wolverine."

"He's cute," Alexandra admitted, watching the antics of the creature the team had adopted as its mascot.

For a few moments, Clif froze as the crowd turned his way and began cheering. Then he remembered his reflection in the mirror. His own aunt wouldn't be able to recognize him in this getup. Prancing toward the first section in the stadium, he waved to the crowd and felt a little thrill of excitement at his duplicity. Turning toward the locker room, he saw Tony watching him. With a shrug, he lifted his hand in a salute. There was no turning back.

As Wooly did at every game, he picked up someone's baby, dressed in the team colors, and twirled him around before planting a kiss on his pudgy cheek and handing him back to his parents. That wasn't difficult; it was easy. In fact, Clif thought, it was fun. There was something exhilarating about being completely anonymous. He glanced around the stands, searching for his next quarry. He patted a fat man on his bald head, then had the crowd roaring with laughter as he offered the victim of his joke a team hat, complete with painted feathers.

As he advanced to their section, Charley joined the crowd of waving, cheering fans. "He's coming this way. Mom, wave at Wooly."

Handing an excited little boy a team banner, Clif accepted his sticky handshake, and realized he was actually having a good time. For the next hour Clif Andrews didn't exist. Assuming the persona of Wooly the Wolverine, he could relax and mingle with ordinary people without the fear of being singled out as the son and grandson of famous men. Though he had fond memories of his father and grandfather, the legacy they'd left him was at times an awesome burden. The role he'd been thrust into as president of Andrews Motors made it difficult for Clif to find the privacy he cherished.

A white-haired woman pumped his hand, then impulsively hugged him. Touching a furry paw to his mouth, he blew a kiss to the crowd. As he waved to the next section, his hand stopped in midair. One face in the front row arrested his attention. All the people around her faded to a blur.

If it weren't for the color of her hair, he'd have sworn it was someone else. But the tangled curls tumbling about her face and shoulders were unmistakable. Her green eyes were filled with laughter. Her cheeks were flushed from the sting of the autumn air. Her eyebrows and the spiky sweep of her lashes glinted gold in the sunlight. Instead of a tailored suit, she wore brown corduroy slacks, a white turtleneck and a brown suede jacket that showed off her trim figure to its best advantage. Oh, yes. This was definitely the very proper Miss Alexandra Porter. But she bore no resemblance to the woman he'd seen in the executive boardroom when he'd appointed her manager of Division Two.

Clif's imagination raced. As long as he was protected by this ridiculous costume, he thought with a wicked grin, he was going to have some fun with her.

He took a step closer, and the little girl beside her clutched her arm. Noticing her for the first time, he reached into his pocket and withdrew a banner. Making a deep bow before the little girl, he presented her with his gift. A look of disbelief crossed her face before she accepted it. Then, throwing her arms around his neck, she hugged him fiercely.

"Oh, Wooly, thank you."

"You're welcome." Bending to her ear, he whispered, "You and your sister are the prettiest girls at the game."

Her eyes widened. Covering her hand with her mouth, she giggled, then looked up at the woman beside her, who was watching with a look of amusement.

"What did he say?"

Before Charley could reply, Clif handed Alexandra a pennant.

"Thank you," she murmured, offering her hand.

Her palm was engulfed in a huge fur-covered paw. Leaning closer, he whispered, "Wooly prefers kisses to handshakes." Before she could refuse, he drew her to him and covered her mouth with his.

He had a quick impression of her haunting fragrance as he brought her against him. On her mouth lingered the sweet tang of soda. And then all he could taste was her, dark and deep and mysterious. Her lips were soft, so soft and pliant he wanted to crush them. The hands that gripped his arms were surprisingly strong. There was depth here and strength, and something he couldn't quite fathom.

The kiss caught her completely off guard. For one brief moment her hands hung limply at her sides. Then she brought them to his arms and curled her fingers into the

plush fur. Beneath the costume she felt the ripple of muscle. With his painted whiskers and garishly smiling mouth,
she'd expected a bland, impulsive kiss. What she found instead was a man's strength. Incredible strength. And carefully contained tension.

Alexandra was a woman who had made a firm promise to
herself. Her head would always rule her heart. She prided
herself on being firm and decisive. She had always been able
to reason her way through any situation. But her reaction to
this simple kiss puzzled her.

Her heart was beating so wildly she could feel her pulse
throb in her temples. Despite the chill in the air, her flesh
heated at his touch. She was hot and cold and very close to
trembling.

Reluctantly he drew back. He watched her take a deep
breath to steady herself. He saw a quick look of stunned
surprise before her eyes flashed fire.

Peering into the slate-gray eyes behind the mask, she had
the unnerving sensation that she'd seen them before. Cool.
Calculating. Arrogant. She shook her head, sending her hair
dancing about her shoulders. Impossible. She would never
forget eyes like those.

With a formal little bow, he turned away and bounded
onto the edge of the field. Moments later a touchdown was
scored, and the crowd erupted into a deafening roar. Wooly
turned. Alexandra was still watching him. With a casual air
he dropped his hand into his pocket, searching for another
pennant. When he withdrew it, he realized it was trembling
slightly. He wanted to blame it on the autumn breeze, but he
knew better. Her mere touch had left his hand unsteady.

For Alexandra, the rest of the game was a blur of color
and noise and taste. All of these, though she'd experienced
them many times before, seemed new and excitingly different. What had transpired between her and that . . . crea-

ture...had no bearing on the excitement of the day, she told herself. A single kiss couldn't make the air sweeter or the day sharper. No, the reason for her thrill of pleasure was that this time she was sharing everything with Charley. And through her daughter's eyes, she felt the lure of the game.

At halftime they ate their way through a small pizza, then topped it off with chocolate-chip ice-cream bars. Wandering around the stadium, they stopped to admire the dozens of souvenirs bearing the team name and colors.

"How about a sweatshirt?" Alexandra asked.

She saw her daughter's eyes widen. "You mean it?"

"Sure. Why not? Do you want the one with the team name, or the one with the picture of Wooly?" she asked, as if she didn't know.

"Wooly," Charley said decisively.

The girl behind the booth reached under the counter and handed them a green-and-gold sweatshirt. Eagerly Charley slipped off her jacket and pulled it on over her T-shirt.

"How do I look?"

Accepting her change, Alexandra couldn't help laughing. "Like a leprechaun. The color is perfect on you."

"Mom." The word was drawn out as only Charley could say it. "I mean, do I look like part of the cheering section?"

"Definitely. They'll think you come to every game."

With a satisfied smile, Charley followed her mother back to their seats.

During the final half they munched pretzels and chips, washing everything down with two large root beers.

They cheered frantically as the Wolverines tied the score, then screamed until they were hoarse when one of the players kicked a field goal to win the game. With the rest of the festive home-team crowd, they made their way through the parking lot and drove home through the gathering shadows of a perfect autumn evening.

"This was the best day ever, Mom," Charley said, taping the Wolverine banner to the wall over her bed. The brightly colored sweatshirt was draped over her chair. It would be worn proudly to school the next morning, the object of her classmates' envy.

Pulling back the covers, Charley slid between the warm flannel sheets. "I wish we could do this every Sunday."

"If we did it every week, it wouldn't be special anymore. Besides, we'd each weigh a ton." Brushing her lips over Charley's cheek, Alexandra chuckled. "Not to mention the strain on the budget. But it was fun. A lot more fun than I'd expected."

"And we got to meet Wooly." Charley giggled suddenly. "He thought we were sisters."

"Hmm. Is that what he whispered to you? Well, I could have corrected him on that, but . . . I got sidetracked."

"Yeah. He kissed you. He only hugged me." Charley's lashes swept up; her eyes were suddenly bright. "What did it feel like to kiss Wooly?"

Alexandra crossed the room and paused in the doorway. The mere mention of that kiss sent her pulse leaping. "Ever kiss a frog?" she quipped.

"That bad, huh?"

"Good night, pumpkin."

"That's pumpkin head, to you."

Still chuckling, Alexandra made her way downstairs to the kitchen. Putting the kettle on for tea, she bundled her robe about her as she settled into a chair.

She couldn't remember the last time she'd felt so disturbed by a simple kiss. Of course, she reasoned, it wasn't so simple. It had been short, lasting only brief seconds. And it had been very public. She'd even been vaguely aware of shouts and laughter going on around her. But it hadn't been simple. It wasn't only his lips, which had aroused her with a single touch. It wasn't only the surprising strength she'd felt in him. It was the chemistry. She'd never before experienced anything like it. That stupid, silly kiss had completely unraveled her nerves.

She jumped when the kettle whistled, then took a steadying breath. When the tea was made, she carried a cup upstairs and set it on her night table beside the alarm clock. Dropping her robe on the foot of the bed, she rummaged through her drawer. Once, in a fit of maternal bliss, she'd bought a pair of beige classically tailored pajamas. They fit her image of the proper mother. They lay in the bottom of her drawer, still wrapped in tissue. It comforted her to know they were there if she ever wanted to wear them. As always, she ignored them and chose instead a brief teddy. It was made up of little bits of pale pink lace, tied at each shoulder, with the merest dusting of lace at each thigh. Slipping it on, she studied her reflection in the mirror. She needed this reassurance. Where had the years gone? she wondered. When had she become so immersed in motherhood and her career that she had completely forgotten her need to be a woman? Why was it that she felt free to indulge herself only in these few private rituals? The woman in the mirror, with her hair flowing about her shoulders, her figure provocatively displayed, was a well-kept secret.

With a sigh she slid between the scented sheets and sipped her tea. She'd had to put aside the luxuries to deal with life's necessities. Still, she didn't feel deprived, she reminded herself. All of it had been her choice. There had been options. Oh, she'd been made aware of her options. She set the cup down with a clatter and plumped her pillow. The goals she'd set for herself eight years ago were the same ones she aspired to now. To raise her daughter. To carve a niche for herself in the business world. To earn back the respect of those she'd shamed. To prove that she was sensible and dependable and worthy of trust.

Snapping off the light, she snuggled beneath the covers and closed her eyes. The thought of that kiss crept unbidden to her mind. She fought to ignore the tiny current that pulsed through her veins. That kiss, though quick and public, had stirred a simmering passion she'd thought long dead. Had it only been dormant these past years, waiting for something or someone to prod it back to life? The thought of those eyes haunted her. Gray. Cold. Intimidating. Yet vaguely familiar. They were the last thing she thought of as she drifted off to sleep.

Chapter Three

"Mom, I can't find my gym shoes."

"Look under your bed."

"I did."

"Check the laundry room." Alexandra clenched her teeth as she wrapped Charley's sandwich and dropped an apple in the brown lunch bag. She should have done this last night. Now she was running late.

Mondays. Why did there have to be a Monday in every week?

"I found one of them."

"Where?"

"Under the sofa cushion."

Of course. Why hadn't she thought of that? "The other has to be there somewhere. Where were you and Milly practicing your ballet?"

"Found it," came the muffled reply. "It was in the flower pot."

It figured. Milly thought the huge clay pots were catchalls. "I'm going out to start the car. Your lunch is on the table."

As Alexandra stepped outside, she felt a bite in the air. There had been a heavy frost during the night. It sparkled on the fiery branches of the trees and dusted the rooftops. Starting the engine, she searched the glove compartment for a scraper and began clearing the windshield.

"Oh." Charley paused on the front step. "The yard looks like cotton candy."

"Looks are deceiving," Alexandra muttered, searching her pockets for her gloves.

"Let me do this side."

Gratefully she handed the scraper to her daughter. With the windows clear, they bundled into the car, eager for its warmth.

Headlights and plumes of frosty exhaust emissions made an eerie pattern on the crowded expressway. They inched their way along until they reached the exit for Charley's school.

"I might be late tonight, honey. This is my first division meeting. I have no idea what to expect. Give my apology to Millicent. And ask her to stay to dinner, if she'd like."

"Okay. Only it's 'Milly' now. She'd decided Millicent is too elegant for her tastes. Bye, Mom."

With a quick kiss, Charley slammed the car door and hurried up the steps to join her friends.

Sometimes it didn't seem fair, Alexandra thought, heading back onto the expressway. She'd never been there when her daughter came in from school. Parent-teacher meetings and school plays were sandwiched in between paperwork brought from the office and housework that never seemed to get done. Thank heavens for Milly, she thought. That generous woman always managed to do more than she was paid to do. Alexandra thought of the special dinners, the times Milly just happened to bake too many cookies or cupcakes and asked Charley and Alexandra to share them with her.

As she parked in the company lot and made her way to her office, Alexandra pushed aside her worries about home. For the next eight hours, all her concentration would be on Andrews Motors.

As she made her way along the hall, workers poked their heads out of offices to congratulate her. The official news of her promotion had been posted earlier. And it sounded as if her assistant had told everyone he'd seen.

"Your phone's been ringing since I took off my coat," Mike said, looking up from his desk. "You even got a call from the Ice Man himself."

He saw Alexandra's quick frown before she flipped through her messages. When she began dialing the phone, he walked out of her office. A few minutes later he returned with a cup of black coffee, which he placed in front of her. She gave him a grateful smile as he leaned his hip against her desk and waited.

"What did the great one want?"

"To meet me in an hour."

"What about?"

"He didn't say. I guess if you're the president, you don't have to give a reason."

Mike grinned. "Maybe he wants to thank you for supporting his team. How'd you like the seats?"

"Oh, Mike. They were wonderful. I had no idea we'd be in the front row."

We. His interest sharpened. "How did your . . . guest enjoy them?"

Alexandra smothered a chuckle. Although he'd been very circumspect, Mike had tried every trick he knew to find out something about her personal life. She had carefully resisted any intrusion. Her life away from the office was strictly off limits.

"How could anyone not enjoy a day like that? Front row seats and a win for the home team. Thanks again, Mike."

Picking up the phone, she effectively cut off any further questions. Clapping her hand over the receiver, she whispered, "Let's call the division meeting for three o'clock. That way I'll have this meeting with the president out of the way first, and have time to prepare an agenda."

He nodded, leaving to make the necessary calls.

At exactly ten o'clock Alexandra rode the elevator to the executive offices. The walls were paneled in rich dark walnut; the carpet was a muted shade of beige. Except for the ringing of a telephone and the click of a word processor, it was as quiet as a church. She found herself wanting to whisper.

The woman behind the desk reminded Alexandra of her eighth-grade teacher. A cap of blue-tinted curls framed a round face that bore the merest trace of makeup. The eyes behind her wire-framed glasses were a clear sparkling blue. There would be no mandatory retirement for the president's secretary.

The woman's smile was warm, genuine. "Miss Porter." Seeing Alexandra's lifted eyebrow, she explained, "I recognize you from your photograph. I'm Martha James."

"Hello, Ms. James."

"Call me Martha." Alexandra felt the strength in the woman's handshake. "Mr. Andrews directed me to show you right in." She skirted her desk and opened the double doors. "He has a long-distance call at the moment. Make yourself comfortable."

For long moments Alexandra stared around her. The president's office occupied one half of the top floor. A wall of glass wrapped around three sides, offering a breathtaking view of Detroit as Alexandra had never seen it.

An ivory tower, she thought. From this height the buildings, streets and riverfront were dwarfed. The traffic jams, the grime, the noise were so far removed that they ceased to exist. From here, Detroit was contemporary steel structures mingling with restored brick buildings, towering church spires and sunlight glinting off a river of glass.

The furnishings were sleek, contemporary pieces, with two leather sofas in gray facing each other across a mirrored table. The small sculpture on the table was a Calder, in vivid red and black. Smiling, she touched it before inspecting further. On mirrored pedestals situated to take advantage of the natural light were larger sculptures. Making a slow, circular tour, Alexandra studied a bronze torso by Rodin. Moving on, she identified a bronze horse and rider as an Aitken. A wood carving of a bust of a young boy stood in a place of honor in front of one of the floor-to-ceiling windows. There was no signature. The sculptor was unknown to her. The light spilling on the piece revealed fine hair, high aristocratic cheekbones, a proudly tilted head. She recognized that boy. Turning, she studied the man behind the desk. Even in his youth, he'd revealed to the artist an aura of power.

In front of the desk were two swivel chairs in gray, black and red. Choosing the one on the left, she sat down and crossed her legs, waiting for an end to the telephone conversation.

Clif was aware of her from the moment she walked in. While the voice on the other end droned on, he watched her make a slow appraisal of his office.

Her reaction to the Calder pleased him. It was a whimsical piece, meant to entertain. The vivid colors cheered him even on the dreariest days.

He saw her reach out a hand to the Aitken. There was fire there, intensity. The man's genius seemed to fascinate her, as it always fascinated him.

And then there was the wood carving. A smile touched his lips. He had been his grandmother's favorite subject. In her lifetime she had done four different sculptures of him.

"No, Arthur, I can't tell you how long before you can start production. The last test wasn't satisfactory. I won't give my approval until I'm certain it will pass the emission tests. As soon as I know, you'll know."

He studied her plain leather pumps, her slender ankles. His gaze moved up her shapely legs to the hem of a navy wool skirt. There was the merest hint of lace visible beneath it. He felt an itch to see more, to touch her, and clenched his fist.

"Thanks, Arthur. I will. Give my best to Lillian."

Replacing the receiver, he leaned back in his chair. "Good morning, Miss Porter."

"Good morning."

He'd forgotten that voice—liquid honey pouring over his senses. His fingers tightened on the arms of the chair.

"Have you called a division meeting?"

"After lunch. My assistant is notifying the department heads right now."

Just listening to her made him feel good. What would she think if he closed his eyes and ordered her to recite the alphabet? The thought made him want to laugh.

"Fine. I have a full schedule today, but I'd like to attend. If I'm free, I'll drop by."

There was something familiar about Clif Andrews. Alexandra studied the Saville Row suit, the carefully knotted silk tie. She'd grown up with men who dressed as well as he, but not too many wore their clothes with such casual elegance. It wasn't the deep voice, the curt delivery. The tone of his voice told her he was a man accustomed to giving or-

ders and having them followed. His was a unique voice, one
she wouldn't forget. But it wasn't his voice. There was
something else vaguely familiar about him. She couldn't put
her finger on it.

"One more thing."

She tensed.

"As a member of midlevel management, you'll be
expected to represent your division at the monthly management assembly. You report to...?"

"Dave Francis."

He seemed to pause a moment. Dave Francis had a reputation for making things tough for newcomers. "Good
man. Dave supports his people. And Dave reports to Frank
Tuller, who in turn sits on the board."

The pecking order. Alexandra was aware that she was a
small cog in the wheel of Andrews Motors. She was also
aware that she had just lost another evening of leisure. One
night a month, she would have to stay at the office through
dinner for a meeting.

All of this could have been said on the telephone. Alexandra found herself wondering why the president of the
company had sent for her.

"If you have any problems, problems that can't be solved
by Dave or Tuller, I want you to come to me."

He said it so quietly that she wondered for a moment if
she'd heard correctly.

"Thank you. I'm sure Dave and I can work together."

"Yes. Of course. But remember my offer." He stood.
"Thanks for stopping by, Miss Porter. If there's time, I'll
see you this afternoon."

She accepted his outstretched hand and felt the jolt. She
hadn't imagined it that first time. It was happening again.

She could feel his cool gaze on her as she walked across
the room and opened the door. When it closed, she rubbed
her damp hand on her skirt, vainly trying to erase his touch.

Mike looked up with interest when she entered her office.

"Well? What did he want?"

She shrugged, uncomfortable about the meeting, yet unable to say why. "Just wanted to welcome me to the family."

"Uh-huh. What else?"

"Nothing important. Maybe he just wanted to look me over."

Mike grinned. "Can't blame a guy for that."

Her head lifted. Mike recognized the movement. Joke time was over. She was all business.

"I was expecting a preliminary report on the catalytic conversion before the division meeting this afternoon. Where is it?"

"Campbell said he'd bring it with him."

"I want it now. Call him."

She turned away and touched an intercom button. "Liz, would you bring your book, please? I have some dictation."

The meeting was going badly. Alexandra wasn't certain just when or how she'd lost control. While she waited for a chance to interrupt, Mike argued with Bill Campbell about quality control. She realized Mike was only trying to run interference for her. Still, she resented it. It was her fight, and she was spoiling to win it. The only problem was that she wasn't even being allowed to spar.

Rapping her hand on the table, she tried vainly to restore order.

"Mike, I have a few questions of my own."

"... put my initials on an order, you can damn well bet I've given it my personal attention."

"Bill. Please. You've made your point. Now if you'll let ..."

"Then how do you explain this slipup?" Mike demanded. Clenching a fistful of papers, Mike waved them under Bill's nose.

"I can't explain it. The mistake didn't come from my department." Bill Campbell's voice thundered around the room.

"All right, gentlemen." Alexandra fought the urge to slam a palm against the table. "I want you both to cool down before you say another word. Do you understand me?"

The two men stood facing each other, hands on hips, eyes narrowed in anger. When the door to the conference room opened, no one even bothered to glance up.

"Bill, after the meeting, I'd like to speak with you in my office." Seeing Mike's mouth open, she snapped, "Alone."

"I have every right..."

"At this moment, Mike, you have no rights. I have the floor."

The two men glared at each other for a moment longer, then turned away to take their seats on opposite sides of the table. It was only after they were seated that a hushed silence fell over the room. Even before she saw Clif Andrews seated at the end of the table, Alexandra felt his presence. Power. It radiated from him in waves, intimidating, silencing even the most vocal critics.

"Emmet." Alexandra's voice softened as she addressed the man who had been her first boss at Andrews Motors. "I read your report on the new paint tests. It's impressive. Why don't you tell us about your findings?"

The old man rose slowly with the aid of a cane. An industrial accident years ago had left him with a withered leg and a legacy of pain each time the weather changed. Nothing could dim his sharp mind or his passion for the machine that had caused his disability.

His head was bald except for a small cap of gray hair. A cigar jutted perpetually from the corner of his mouth. No one had ever seen him light it. His suit was rumpled. He'd loosened the knot of his tie. Removing a pile of folded notes from his breast pocket, he smoothed them with his fingers, removed the cigar from his mouth and began reading.

Clif leaned back, watching Alexandra. He'd stood outside the door, listening to the voices raised in anger. His first inclination had been to charge inside and put an end to the argument. Then he'd thought better of it. This was her first division meeting. They were testing her. If he ran interference this time, they would simply wait until the first time she was alone. Better to let her jump in with both feet. It was her show. He'd let her run it her way.

While Emmet delivered the report, Clif studied the woman at the head of the table. She wore her new title well. Though her personnel file showed that she had started at Andrews Motors while she was still in college, working her way up from the lowest-paying position, there was an aura of sophistication and breeding about her. It was obvious in the way she wore her clothes, in that haughty voice. It was there in her walk; she had the loose-limbed sleek movement of a thoroughbred. There was something intriguing about the aloof Miss Porter. There was much more to her than brains and looks. The woman had style.

Alexandra glanced at her watch. The meeting had gone longer than she'd expected. These people were as eager as she to get home.

"Thank you, Emmet. If the final tests go as well as the preliminary ones, I'd say we've finally found the finish we've been searching for all these years. It may even be impervious to road salt. Wouldn't that make the consumer cheer?"

Everyone nodded.

"In case anyone hasn't noticed," Alexandra said with a smile, "our president, Mr. Andrews, joined us a while ago. Mr. Andrews, is there anything you might like to add before we adjourn?"

Clif remained seated. "Nothing, Miss Porter. You seem to have handled everything."

She moistened her lips. "Bill, I'll see you in my office. Mike, you may as well go home. We can talk tomorrow morning." She glanced around the room. "Thank you all, ladies and gentlemen. Good night."

As Bill Campbell picked up his report and headed toward her office, her assistant watched him with a scowl. Then, snatching up his own copy of the report, he stormed out of the conference room. The others filed out, cowed into silence by the presence of the president.

Playing for time, Alexandra shuffled her reports, stacking them neatly then placing them in a file folder for her secretary. She was uncomfortably aware that the president was still seated at the conference table, watching her. Had he heard the raised voices? Was he already questioning his choice of division manager?

When she turned, he uncoiled himself from the chair. They both reached the door at the same time.

He reached for the handle, effectively stopping her. "I'd like a full report tomorrow on this business between Mike and Bill."

She glanced at the hand that barred her way, then nodded. "As soon as I've sorted it out."

He inhaled the earthy scent of her perfume. "You handled yourself well in here."

"Thank you, Mr. Andrews."

"Clif."

Taken by surprise, she said quickly, "I think not. I prefer Mr. Andrews."

She glanced up and found herself staring into cool gray eyes. Calculating, arrogant eyes. In that instant something clicked in her mind. She let out a little gasp and covered her mouth with her hand.

"It can't be. You!" The file folder dropped from her nerveless fingers, spilling papers about their feet. Neither of them seemed to notice.

Her voice was barely more than a whisper. "I know those eyes." How could she have missed it? Those stern penetrating eyes, had been so at odds with the whimsical creature the fans were cheering.

"Do you now?" His eyebrow arched in that intimidating way. He brought his other hand up, pinning her against the door.

"I know I'm not mistaken. I could never forget those eyes." She licked her lips. Her voice lowered as the words came out in a rush. "You're that mascot. Wooly."

His eyes narrowed. Damn his luck. Why had he allowed himself to get close enough to her to be recognized? His mouth tightened to a thin white line. A little pulse throbbed in his temple. "Very astute, Ms. Porter. But I'm not the mascot. I just pretended to be him briefly. I . . . was paying off a bet."

"Of course." She gave him a measured look. "You lost a bet."

He could see amusement sparkle in her eyes. "I don't owe you an explanation."

"You most certainly don't." A smile tugged at the corner of her lips. She bit it back.

He swore. "I never expected anyone to guess my identity. I'm certain you'll understand that it must remain our little secret."

She searched his stiff features. The president of Andrews Motors prancing about the field in a wolverine costume while his team played football. Unthinkable. It would make great copy for the gossip magazines, Alexandra thought. But it could destroy the credibility of the president of Andrews Motors.

He watched the gleam in her eye. She was laughing. Behind that beautiful mask of composure, she was laughing at the thought of him in that costume.

Nibbling on her lower lip, she nodded. "I assure you that I can be trusted to keep your secret."

His frown deepened. "You'd better. I've already threatened the real mascot if he leaks even a whisper. The same goes for you, Miss Porter. One word, and I'll have your head." His gaze slid over her hair. His tone softened. "Such a pretty head." Suddenly he smiled. It was the first time she'd seen that wicked smile, a smile that did unsettling things to her nerves. A man who could laugh—at himself, at the world—intrigued her. Just how many other little surprises was he hiding?

A new thought left her suddenly stricken. Her eyes widened with the realization. "Mr. Andrews, you took advantage of me. You . . . kissed me. You were laughing at me."

"Wrong, Miss Porter." He was standing so close to her that she could smell the clean lemony scent of his soap. "I never laughed at you. I was simply enjoying the fans and their jokes. I was laughing with them. And that kiss." His tone lowered abruptly. "That kiss . . ." She saw his gaze fall on her mouth. "Frankly, it was very public and very unsatisfactory. I'd like to try again."

He moved closer, still not touching her. She stiffened, afraid to move, afraid even to breathe. She mustn't let him do this. She had to stop him now, before he touched her. Still she waited, as if frozen to the spot.

He saw the fear in her eyes. It wasn't the effect he usually had on women, he thought, puzzled. She drew back against the door, vainly trying not to touch him with any part of her

body. She seemed absolutely terrified. The more she resisted, the more tempting she became.

"I believe the word was *kiss*. I wasn't planning to beat
you, Miss Porter. I don't usually flog my employees, publicly or privately." She heard the warmth of humor in his
tone.

Deliberately bending nearer, he inhaled the exotic spicy
fragrance that was uniquely hers. He saw her eyes widen,
then shut tightly.

His warm breath feathered the hair at her temple. His
words whispered over her senses, leaving her breathless.
"Open your eyes, Miss Porter."

Her lids fluttered, then opened wide.

In that brief instant, he felt a sexual pull that clawed at his
insides. One touch. That would be enough to satisfy his
craving for her. One kiss, and he would be willing to walk
away.

His gaze scanned her silken hair, her flawless skin. Who
was he kidding? One tiny touch, and he would be lost. One
kiss from those lips would never be enough. Even now, just
standing close enough to inhale her perfume, to feel the
warmth of her breath on his cheek, he wanted it all. If he
took even a single step closer, it would be too late to turn
back.

Alexandra felt the tension in every part of her body. She
watched Clif with a kind of terrible fascination. The electricity that sizzled between them was so strong, so compelling that they were both being burned by it. She didn't want
this. Smoldering passion terrified her. She'd put aside these
needs long ago and learned to channel her energy into a
drive that she could control—the drive to succeed.

Battling his own desire, Clif stared down into her eyes and
watched as they hardened. She lifted her chin, a sure sign
that she was once again in control.

"If you'll excuse me, Mr. Andrews, I have an employee waiting in my office." The breathy tone of her voice told him what it cost her to speak. "I've kept him waiting long enough."

"This isn't over, Miss Porter."

She blinked. She'd hoped this little incident could be put aside. They'd come close, very close to something dangerous. "Oh, but it is. And I'm sure you'll be gentleman enough to keep your distance."

"Don't bet on it."

She shot him a murderous look, then glanced down. For a moment she stared at the papers at their feet as if she'd forgotten them. Then, dropping to her knees, she began snatching up the scattered papers. Kneeling beside her, Clif picked up the rest and handed them to her. She accepted them without looking at him.

As she strode away, Clif watched the way she kept her spine stiff. The sway of her hips caused a rush of heat that surprised him.

He'd glimpsed something in her eyes that stunned him. He hadn't expected vulnerability. Alexandra Porter seemed so poised. Cool and emotionless. Perfection. That was the word that came to mind whenever he thought of her. And he'd found himself thinking of her too often lately.

Leaning against the wall, he listened to the sound of her high heels in the silent hallway. He'd just had an intimate glimpse below the polished surface of the prim Miss Porter. And it was obvious she resented it. Could it be, he wondered, shaking a cigarette from a pack, that she was afraid of what he'd find?

Chapter Four

There's definitely a leak."

Frank Tuller held aloft the latest edition of *Wheels Magazine*. The board members seated around the table listened intently. Their grim faces revealed their concern.

"The facts and figures quoted in this article came directly from our monthly report on auto emissions tests. That report hasn't even been circulated among the other divisions within the company."

"You mean the leak is within Division Two?" Clif accepted the copy of the magazine and scanned the contents of the article being discussed.

"It has to be," Tuller said vehemently. "No one else has access to this information."

"According to this article, our company is scrambling to make our latest engine prototype measure up to the Environmental Protection Agency's requirements." Clif looked up sharply. "Is that true?"

Tuller flushed under the icy scrutiny. "It's tight. But we're not worried. We're this close to compliance." He held his thumb and finger slightly apart.

"It's obvious to me," Marion broke in, "that heads ought to roll, beginning with the new manager." She'd been seething ever since she'd heard about a promotion that had occurred while she was out of town.

"She's only been on the job a few weeks," Clif said.

"That's enough time to leak test results." Marion sat straighter, enjoying the spotlight.

"And if the leaks continue," Clif said quietly, "do we just keep on firing our top people, hoping the guilty party is among them?"

"I think we should launch a full-scale investigation," Tuller interjected.

"And I think we should make an example of someone." Marion lifted a glass of ice water to her lips. "I resent anyone who tries to muddy the name of Andrews Motors."

"A feeling we all share." Clif strove to keep his temper in check. "If the board will approve, I'd like to handle this myself. I'll hire a discreet investigator. I'd prefer to keep it from becoming a full-blown scandal."

"I agree," one of the vice presidents said quickly, eager to catch his plane to the coast. "Clif is certainly closer to the daily situation than the rest of us. If you're willing to take on one more dirty job, Clif, I'm on your side."

Around the table, heads nodded in agreement.

"I'll put it in the form of a motion," the vice president said.

As the secretary took notes, the votes were tallied.

When the board meeting broke up, Marion stalked her nephew to his office. Closing the door behind her, she leaned against it and watched as he walked to his desk.

"You don't seem worried about the leak."

Clif studied his aunt. Her latest trip to the spa had left her lean, tanned and fit. In fighting form, he thought tiredly. "Oh, but I am, Marion."

"Then why don't you start cracking the whip?"

"Because," he said patiently, "we haven't even hitched the mule to the cart yet."

"I don't care for your humor, Clif."

He smiled. Marion, in her pink cashmere suit, her hair a carefully arranged beige confection, could never be accused of possessing a sense of humor. "Division Two has over a hundred employees. They're all involved in testing programs. Any one of them could leak the test results to outside interests."

"But the wording of the article was taken directly from a secret report. Only management had access to that."

Clif rubbed a weary hand over his eyes. "That narrows it down to a dozen or so suspects. I'll find the one responsible."

Marion clenched her hands at her sides. "If I were in charge..."

"I know, Marion," Clif said, interrupting. "You'd cut off their heads."

Her lips thinned.

Clif was grateful for the ringing of his telephone.

"Excuse me." Lifting the phone, he swiveled his chair. When he heard the closing of his office door, he gave a sigh. "Thank you, Martha. I swear sometimes you can read my mind."

His elderly secretary laughed. "I could see the fire in your aunt's eyes. I knew you were in for a long session if I didn't come to the rescue."

"Bless you. Have the notices about the monthly management assembly gone out?"

"They're being hand delivered right now."

"Fine. Bring in your notebook, Martha. I'd like to dictate a few memos for the meeting tonight."

Mike waved the notice in front of Alexandra. "Monthly management assembly tonight. Are you going?"

Alexandra read the memo and sighed. "Looks like I have no choice."

Leaning his hip against her desk, he said casually, "I swear I've seen the Ice Man skulking around this department more in the past few weeks than he has in two years."

"I don't think the president of the company can be accused of skulking," she said with a laugh.

"What would you call it?"

"Showing an interest." She bent over a drawer and fumbled with a file folder to avoid Mike's gaze.

The truth was, she, too, had begun to question the man's frequent visits to her department. Every time she turned around, Clif Andrews seemed to be following her. He was always businesslike. But his very presence intimidated her. Ever since their encounter in the conference room, she'd gone out of her way to avoid him. Tonight, she promised herself, would be no exception.

One of the managers had told Alexandra what to expect at her first monthly managerial meeting. There would be a buffet supper, during which the upper management mingled with the department heads. The business meeting would consist mainly of a progress report from each division, followed by a discussion of any problems they should be aware of. The meeting usually broke up around ten o'clock.

Promptly at six o'clock, Alexandra entered the conference room and stood in line for the buffet. Thinking about the wonderful stew Milly had made the previous night, she helped herself to a salad and roll and made her way to the coffee urn.

"When I retire," a stocky man muttered beside her, "I'd like to get the coffee concession for this place. Bet I'd make a million."

Alexandra nodded. "If the company ever ran out of coffee, most of the employees would resign in protest."

"I'd be first in line," came a deep voice behind her.

Turning, she found herself looking into the solemn eyes of Clif Andrews.

"Good evening, Mr. Andrews."

"Good evening, Miss Porter. Where are you sitting?"

He could read the discomfort in her eyes. "Anywhere there's room."

"Follow me." He picked up his tray and threaded his way through the tables to one that was nearly empty.

Alexandra had no choice but to follow.

"How's your job working out?" he asked casually as he buttered a roll.

"Fine." She wondered if the other managers had noticed that he'd singled her out.

"No problems?"

Alexandra thought about the copy of *Wheels Magazine* she'd found on her assistant's desk. She was still too upset about the lead article to discuss it. The report had been taken practically verbatim from a top-secret report circulated in their division. She lifted a fork. "None I can't handle."

Clif thought he detected a slight hesitation. Giving her his full attention, he asked, "Nervous about your first managerial report?"

"Should I be?"

"Not at all. Nobody here bites." In a softer tone he added, "Although we do touch lips when we're able."

Alexandra's face turned several shades of pink. Just then several other people joined them, preventing her from making a comment she might have regretted later. Clif smoothly shifted his attention to include the others, although he was acutely aware of the woman beside him.

By the time most of the people had returned from the dessert table, the business meeting began. After a brief statement from the president on profit and loss, each division head was called to the microphone for a report. Alexandra's went smoothly. She spoke about the tests on the newest engine prototypes, which were inching closer to EPA standards, and emphasized the positive results in the paint and chemical department. When she was finished, she was relieved to note that she wouldn't have to field any questions. The next manager took his place at the microphone.

Clif watched her walk to her chair. She had a way of moving, a way of holding her head that said, as plainly as any sign, Keep Away. She'd built a wall around herself, and only the boldest would dare to storm it. He leaned back in his chair as the speaker droned on. A half smile touched the corners of his lips. There was nothing he enjoyed more than a tough challenge. He was going to tear down that wall, brick by brick. He was going to break through to the real Alexandra Porter. And when he did, he intended to know everything there was about this very private lady.

Alexandra slid back her chair slightly. The man in front of her had wide shoulders, preventing a clear view of the speaker's podium. She refused to admit that she wanted to stare at Clif Andrews. She only wanted to memorize the names and faces of all the managers at this meeting, she told herself firmly. While the speaker gave his report she studied the man who presided over the meeting.

Clif Andrews was an enigma. His elegant clothes, his aristocratic bearing, set him apart from all the others. Those cool glances and icy responses to his employees only added to the image of an aloof dictator. Yet the humor she could detect beneath the surface puzzled her. Could it be that there was a heart beating within the ice sculpture?

Their eyes met. It was a moment of shocking intimacy. In that brief instant she felt a touch as strong and compelling as any physical contact. Power. She could feel the power emanating from him. He would be a dangerous adversary. Passion. He was a man of deep passions. She sensed it. He would be an exciting lover.

Her mouth went dry. Where had those thoughts come from? He wasn't her enemy: he was her boss. And she had no intention of taking a lover. Not now. Maybe not ever.

Clif blinked. His thoughts dissolved. Someone had just asked him a question, and he hadn't the faintest idea what it was about. Damn the woman! One look. One simple look, and he was lost. She was destroying his ability to concentrate.

"I'm sorry." He leaned forward toward the microphone at his table on the dais. "Could you repeat the question?"

Clif covered his blunder and carried the meeting to its conclusion. He was relieved when the crowd rose and began making its way through the wide double doors. He glanced at the clock. Ten-thirty. He could probably manage another hour of work in his office.

As he started down the hall, he passed a small knot of employees. He knew without looking that Alexandra Porter was among them. He was developing an extra sense about her.

"We're going to Chuckles for a nightcap, Alexandra. Want to join us?"

He slowed his footsteps to hear her response.

"Not tonight. Got to run. But thanks."

Pausing at the end of the hallway, he watched as she approached. He saw the way she hesitated, saw the look that came into her eyes, then disappeared just as quickly. She was like a rabbit when the headlights of a car momentarily blind it. Her eyes revealed fear mixed with confusion. Then her head lifted in challenge. This was no rabbit, he thought with admiration. And she had no intention of running.

"Need a ride home?" he asked.

"No, thanks." She avoided his eyes.

The light was diffused, touching her face with soft shadows. In the faint illumination her hair was the color of aged brandy. Little tendrils had slipped from the neat knot to kiss her cheeks.

Without thinking, he reached out to touch a strand.

"Silk," he murmured.

He saw her eyes darken to jade.

"Mr. Andrews, I . . ."

"Clif."

Her chin jutted. "Mr. Andrews . . ."

"Clif." His voice hardened. "Say it."

They stood, inches apart. His finger twisted the strand of hair, then tugged until she looked up to meet his dark gaze.

She swallowed. The word came out angry, breathless. "Clif."

He felt a ripple of pleasure. "I like hearing my name on your lips." He bent nearer, inhaling the sweet spicy fragrance that would always remind him of her. "But what I'd really like is having my lips on your lips."

"I'm sorry I can't oblige you." As she began to move away, he caught her by the shoulder and drew her back against the length of him. She was surprised by the strength in his hands.

With his mouth he touched the hair at her temple, and he murmured, "I think you're some kind of witch, Alexandra Porter. You've been distracting me, shattering my concentration." He brushed his lips across her cheek, then pressed them to her ear, sending tiny pinpricks of pleasure along her spine. "Thoughts of you flit through my mind at the oddest times. Lately you've even managed to wake me from a sound sleep."

"I can't be held accountable for your thoughts."

He turned her slowly in his arms until she was facing him. His gaze swept her flushed cheeks, her pursed lips. He ran a fingertip lightly over a feathery eyebrow and saw her frown.

"Indulge me, Miss Porter. I'm not a man usually given to flights of fancy. But the thought of your lips has become something of an obsession."

"Then I suggest a hobby. Race driving, or diving for sunken treasure. I've heard they can become quite obsessive, as well."

"You're a cruel woman, Miss Porter. Do you like playing with my emotions?"

Her voice deepened in anger. She was unaware that the low, husky tone only made her more attractive. "I haven't time to play, Mr. Andrews. And if I did, I wouldn't choose to play with the president of the company."

"Not a president. A mere man, Miss Porter. A man whose heart seems to be betraying him."

Her eyes held him enthralled. He stared down into the purest, clearest green he'd ever seen. A man could drown in those eyes, he realized.

When he looked at her like that, her thoughts scattered. She had to force herself to feel nothing. This couldn't be happening, she thought. Hadn't she done everything in her power to keep the distance between them? Hadn't she resisted every temptation he'd placed in her path? She'd be sorry. Tomorrow, in the office, next week in the conference room, she would have to become even more distant, more aloof. She'd have to— The thought dissolved as his hands gripped her shoulders, drawing her closer, closer to the heat of his body.

A sound of laughter close by caused them both to stiffen. Lifting his head, Clif continued to grip her tightly.

Alexandra realized how vulnerable they both were to company gossip. Pushing a hand to his chest, she struggled to free herself from his grasp and put some distance between them.

"I want to see you somewhere away from the office," he murmured.

"No. I—that's impossible."

"Meet me for a drink."

"I can't."

"Your place?"

"No." Her voice was stronger now. Her mind was clearing. What could she have been thinking of? Stepping back several paces, she stared up at him with a look that was both confused and troubled.

When Emmet lumbered around the corner, struggling to get his arm into his topcoat, she seemed relieved. "Here. Let me help."

She held the coat while he found the armhole. Chomping on his unlit cigar, he gave her a smile of thanks. Glancing at Clif, he grunted, "Meeting ran long tonight."

"Yeah. Sorry about that, Emmet."

The older man shrugged. "Got to keep an eye on that clock. Good night."

"I'll walk with you, Emmet," Alexandra said too brightly. She had no trouble keeping up with his halting, uneven stride.

Clif watched them walk away. Clever lady. It was obvious he made her nervous. But why? Suddenly turning on his heels, he decided to forget the work for tonight. It would still be there in the morning.

In the brightly lighted parking lot, Clif had no trouble spotting Emmet and Alexandra. The old man waited beside his car until she walked to hers and closed the door. Then, turning on the ignition, he drove away.

Clif crossed the lot and unlocked the door of his car, the company's latest model sports car. On the night of the monthly management assembly, he drove himself rather than keep a chauffeur waiting. When Alexandra's car passed him, he eased out of his reserved parking slot and followed.

She was a good driver. That was the first thing he noticed. Of course, anyone who worked with automobiles was expected to be a good driver. But the truth was that many of his employees were surprisingly careless.

They entered the expressway, and she increased her speed. Clif allowed a truck to get between their vehicles. It was bad enough to be following a beautiful woman like a lovesick schoolboy. He certainly didn't want her to catch him at it.

When she left the expressway, he followed more slowly. The neighborhood was familiar. They were only a few miles from his own house. He pulled over and turned off the lights of his car. Up ahead, he watched as she slowed, then turned into a driveway. Waiting until she walked inside, he drove closer.

In the darkness, a single porch light burned, illuminating the front of the house. Her choice of home was intriguing. Yet he had to admit the architecture suited her. It was a blend of sophisticated English Tudor and fairy-tale English castle. The roof was a series of whimsical turrets. He'd seen places like this before. Many of the older estates in the area had such structures on the grounds. Brick-and-stone fortresses standing guard at the entrance to the property. The aloof, mysterious Miss Porter lived in a converted gatehouse.

As he made his way home in the frosty autumn night, a plan began to form in his mind. Surprises. Alexandra Porter was a woman full of surprises. Maybe it was time to confound her with a few of his own.

Chapter Five

Alexandra loved Saturdays. There were no alarms, no schedules. There was time for a second cup of coffee. She sat at the kitchen table with the entire weekend paper spread out in front of her. She was wearing faded jeans and a bright red sweatshirt that read For This I Went to College? It had been Charley's gift to her for Mother's Day. Though she forced herself to read, her thoughts continued to stray to the incident with Clif Andrews. That scene in the hallway had left her more shaken than she cared to admit. What was it about that man? He was the most irritating, the most... fascinating man she'd ever known.

Hearing her daughter's light tread on the stairs, she looked up.

"Isn't it a bit early for ballet practice?"

In her pink tights and leotard, Charley executed a shaky pirouette and reached for the cereal. "Milly's coming over in a little while to bake biscuits, and she said we could do our exercises while they're baking."

"Very clever. Milly intends to kill two birds with one stone."

"Three birds," Charley said, rummaging in the drawer for a spoon. "I'm going to learn how to bake, too. Milly says your mother neglected that part of your education."

Alexandra winced, thinking of her mother's spotless kitchen and the staff of servants who would have been horrified if a little girl had ever intruded on their domain.

"Milly's right. I'm glad she's around to fill in the gaps." Draining the last of her coffee, Alexandra stood. "Does this mean you're not coming to the grocery store with me?"

"Sorry. Next week." She turned. "And Mom, don't forget, it's my turn to push the cart. I'll let you load."

"Thanks a lot." Alexandra picked up her shopping list. "See you in an hour."

On her way out the door, she encountered Milly just coming in. Her housekeeper was wearing purple sweatpants and a baggy purple top. Around her forehead she'd tied a purple sweatband. Little tufts of orange hair drooped over it.

"Serious exercises this morning, hmm?"

Milly nodded. "They're always serious."

"Need anything at the store?"

"Got the list right here."

With a grin Alexandra headed for the car. If it weren't for this thoughtful woman, she and Charley would probably exist on canned soup.

It was a perfect autumn day. The sun filtering through the fiery foliage made a kaleidoscope of patterns on the windshield. The air was brisk, with just a hint of the weather that was to come.

As Alexandra turned into her driveway, she spotted the strange car and wondered who Milly was entertaining this time. Every salesman or poll-taker who knocked on the door was treated like company. Once Alexandra had returned to find two magazine salesmen comfortably ensconced in the living room, sipping tea and munching cookies, while Milly discussed the merits of every magazine on their list. Another time it was a young college student doing a survey. He'd spent nearly three hours in the kitchen, while Milly plied him with sandwiches and milk.

Lifting the heavy sacks of groceries, Alexandra pushed the door open with her hip and entered the kitchen. The aroma of something wonderful wafted from the oven. On the chopping block, Milly had all the ingredients for an exotic omelet. As Alexandra efficiently put away the boxes and cans, she was glad that she hadn't taken the time to eat breakfast. Lunch was going to be special.

"Good. You're back."

Alexandra turned, her eyebrows lifting in surprise. Gone were the purple sweatpants Milly had been wearing just an hour ago. She was now dressed in a long purple tunic over black silk pajama pants.

"What's the occasion?"

Milly brushed an imaginary piece of lint from her shoulder and tried to appear casual. "You mean this old thing? I just thought I'd clean up now that my exercises are over."

As she passed the dining room, Alexandra stopped and backed up. "The table is set with the good china."

"I didn't think you'd mind."

Alexandra eyed her suspiciously. "I don't. Where's Charley?"

"Out back."

"With whom?"

Milly's voice lowered. "Our visitor."

"I hope it's at least a queen or a duke, considering all the fuss you're making."

Milly's eyes twinkled. "Even better than that. It's your boss."

For a moment Alexandra was thunderstruck. Her mouth opened, then clamped shut. Storming to the window, she lifted the curtain. Charley, in her chinos and sweatshirt, was tossing a football to Clif Andrews. Jumping high, he neatly caught it. His T-shirt pulled away from faded denims, displaying a lean, flat stomach. Bringing his arm back, he tossed an easy catch to Charley.

Alexandra found herself staring at a Clif Andrews she'd never seen before. Now that she saw him without his business suit and tie, she was powerfully aware of his trim, athletic body. His shoulders and arms beneath the clinging T-shirt were corded with muscles. His hair was wind-tossed.

Charley's girlish laughter trilled at something he said. The sound of a man's easy, rumbling of laughter was something Alexandra hadn't even known she'd missed until she heard it.

Charley's mouth moved continually as she scooped up the ball and carried it toward Clif. By this time, Alexandra thought with agitation, Charley had probably filled him in on their complete family history, beginning with the early 1900s. Before Charley was through, Clif Andrews would know how many fillings were in her mouth and the birthdate of her pediatrician.

Seeing him glance toward the window, Alexandra quickly dropped the edge of the curtain.

"Why did you let him in, Milly?"

The housekeeper looked up from the stove. "Why wouldn't I? You don't want me to be rude to your boss, do you?"

Alexandra hesitated beside the window, chewing on her lip. Clif had just changed all the rules of the game. In fact, she couldn't even figure out what game he was playing.

"Hey, Mom." Charley burst through the door with Clif following her. "Clif just showed me a neat trick about tossing the football."

"Clif? I see you two are on a first-name basis already."

"I wanted to call her Miss Porter, but she insisted on Charley," he joked.

"Mom," Charley said, drawing out the word. "If you hold the ball with the laces here—" she turned the ball to give her mother a clearer view "—you get a better grip on it. Isn't that neat?"

"Yeah. Neat."

"You don't sound too excited."

"I'm just a little surprised." Over her daughter's head, she studied Clif Andrews. Her voice frosted over. "What are you doing here?"

"Tossing the football to Charley," he said blandly. "She has a good arm."

"That isn't what I mean."

Standing between them, Charley turned from one to the other, watching their expressions.

"Oh, you mean what am I doing in here?" He gave her a lazy smile that did strange things to her heart. "Millicent promised us her special omelets when the game was over."

"Just when is the game over, Mr. Andrews?"

"Clif," he said amiably, then turned toward the kitchen, ignoring her question. "What can I do to help, Millicent?"

"Not one thing," the housekeeper insisted, steering him toward the hallway. "You and Charley wash up. The omelets are done."

So were the waffles with blueberry sauce and walnut topping, Alexandra noted. There was also fresh orange juice and the rich fragrance of Milly's special coffee blend.

"You're sure you haven't stashed a queen or duke in one of the closets?" Alexandra's tone was filled with sarcasm. "Believe me, Milly, Clif Andrews is a mere man."

The housekeeper ignored her as she bustled about, making certain everything was perfect.

"That's a lot of food for four people. Is Mr. Andrews bringing his football team?"

A frown line appeared between Milly's eyes. "Careful. He'll hear you." The frown turned into a brilliant smile as Clif and Charley entered the dining room.

"You sit here, Clif," Charley said, indicating one end of the table. "My mom always sits there." She pointed to the other end. "And Milly and I will sit on each side."

"Isn't this cozy," Alexandra said, giving Clif a look that would kill.

"Just what I was thinking." He took a bite of the omelet and rolled his eyes heavenward. "Millicent, my compliments."

She blushed like a schoolgirl. "You really like it?"

"It may be the best omelet I've ever tasted."

Alexandra watched as Clif poured on the charm. Milly was actually glowing.

"How about the orange juice, Clif?" Charley said between bites. "I squeezed it."

"By hand?" He seemed impressed.

"Well, actually we have an electric thing that squeezes the oranges and spits out the seeds and junk."

He grinned. "It's terrific, Charley."

She beamed.

"And what did you contribute to this meal, Alex?" he asked.

She nearly choked. "Miss Porter," she said through clenched teeth. "And I contributed the money to buy the food you're eating."

"Very creative." His grin widened.

"Clif thought we might like to take a drive to the old cider mill later." Charley's eyes were shining. "He said they have the best cider and doughnuts in the whole world."

"Weren't you planning to go to Tracey's this afternoon?"

"I can do that another time. I already called her and explained that we have company."

Charley made it sound so important that Alexandra was at a loss to think of a graceful way to extricate herself from this situation without hurting her.

"I'm sorry you didn't call first, Mr. Andrews." Alexandra strove for a brightness she didn't feel. "But I'm afraid I've already made a few plans of my own."

Milly reached for the coffeepot. "You told me you were going to clean out the attic." She turned away, completely missing the flush of embarrassment that stole across Alexandra's cheeks. "More coffee, Clif?"

"Thanks, Millicent." He smiled up at her, and she nearly swooned. "That's great coffee."

"My own special blend."

"I'll have to get the recipe from you. I grind my own beans, too, but I've never managed to get this rich taste." He glanced across the table at Alexandra, who sat scowling at him. "If you can tear yourself away from the attic, would you like to join Charley and me this afternoon?"

"Are you suggesting that I would let Charley go somewhere alone with a perfect stranger?"

He gave her a brilliant smile. "I'm really not perfect." Before Alexandra could comment, he added, "And I'm far from a stranger. We'd both love to have you along."

"Come on, Mom," Charley chirped. "We've never been to the cider mill."

"I'll think about it," Alexandra said, "after I've had a chance to speak with Mr. Andrews alone."

"That means she's weakening," Charley said in a stage whisper as she picked up her empty plate and walked to the kitchen.

"Milly," the childish voice called from the other room, "is it my turn to wash the pots and pans?"

"No. Today I wash. You dry." Turning her head, Milly asked, "Can I get you anything else before I go, Clif?"

He gave her a warm smile. "Not a thing, Millicent. Everything was perfect."

Once they were alone, Clif took a moment to study his surroundings. Like Alexandra Porter, her house was full of surprises.

From his vantage point, he could see into the entrance foyer. An early Picasso of a mother and child hung above a red-lacquered Louis XV commode. Miss Porter hadn't bought that on the salary he paid her.

The dining room furniture consisted of a sleek contemporary pedestal table in black lacquer, and matching chairs upholstered in striking black and white. The china was antique. The portrait dominating one wall was of a stunningly beautiful woman with russet hair and emerald eyes.

"Your mother?"

"Grandmother."

"She's beautiful. It seems to be a family trait."

For a moment Alexandra almost smiled. Then she seemed to catch herself. She was not about to waste any warmth on him.

Alexandra sipped her coffee, listening to the chatter coming from the kitchen. Taking a deep breath, she lifted her gaze to the man across the table.

Her words came out in a hiss of anger. "How did you find my house?"

"I find it charming."

"That isn't what I mean, and you know it. How did you find out where I live?"

"I followed you last night."

Her cup clattered against the saucer. She dropped her hands to her lap. They weren't quite steady. "Why?"

"Because I wanted to see you away from the office."

"All right." Her voice was tight, controlled. "You've seen me. You've seen how I live. Satisfied?"

"Not yet."

Her gaze lifted at his low tone. "What else do you want, Mr. Andrews?" She stood, scraping back her chair, and strode to the window. Crossing her arms over her chest, she said, "You've invaded my privacy, barged into my home. You've managed to fool my daughter and housekeeper into thinking you're a combination of the Tooth Fairy and Prince Charming. Is that what you wanted?

He crossed the room to stand in front of her. "I didn't realize when I saw you at the game that Charley was your daughter. I thought you were sisters."

"So now you know."

"I know that you have a delightful daughter and a... unique housekeeper."

"And now will you leave?"

"I'm afraid I can't. There's one more thing I have to know."

She released her breath in a long sigh. She'd been anticipating this. She glanced up. His eyes were hard, his stance rigid, as he studied her revealing features.

She swallowed. She'd show him she was tough enough to face him down. Though she had always gone to great pains to keep her private life private, she had always been scrupulously honest when confronted with tough questions. And this tough question was invariably the first one asked.

Meeting his cold look, she asked, "All right, Mr. Andrews. What else do you want to know?" She braced herself. A band tightened around her heart.

He sensed her fear. It was almost a palpable thing. Thinking quickly, he decided to change tactics. His voice dropped to a low, intimate purr. "I need to know if Millicent is married or single."

A sudden silence stretched between them. Of all the things she was anticipating, this was the most unexpected, off-the-wall question of all.

"Milly?" she sputtered. "Married? No. No, she isn't married. Why do you ask?"

"I think I've fallen in love with her," Clif whispered.

Alexandra collapsed into a fit of laughter. "Milly. You're in love with Milly." The laughter grew until she was nearly doubled over. Tears glimmered, then spilled over as she continued to laugh.

Clif joined in, then touched a thumb to her face as a tear trickled down her cheek. He loved the sound of her laughter. It was a rich, joyous thing.

"You know what they say. In this big world, there's someone for everyone. Now, about that trip to the cider mill..." he began.

"I wouldn't miss it," she said between giggles. "And I'm sure Milly will be delighted. I've never had a chance to play matchmaker before. Charley and I will sit in the back seat."

He caught her by the shoulder and pulled her close. "I'll have to ask you to sit beside me. I don't think I could handle being that close to a woman who can cook like Millicent. I'm afraid I'll lose control. There's no telling what I might do."

She mimicked his serious manner. "Good idea. I'll be happy to act as chaperon."

He inhaled her unique fragrance, and his smile vanished. In those faded denims and that ridiculous sweatshirt she was more appealing than ever. Her hair swung soft and loose about her shoulders. He longed to plunge his hands into it, to draw her firmly against him, to crush her lips with his.

His gaze fastened on her mouth. He saw her eyes widen. "Don't."

"Afraid you'll make Millicent jealous?"

She attempted to smile, but he saw her lips quiver. Without thinking, he touched a fingertip to her mouth and traced the outline of her lips. At his touch her lips parted slightly. She couldn't hide the fear in her eyes.

"Your skin is so soft," he murmured. Lifting his hand, he traced the arch of her eyebrow, the curve of her cheek. She moved her face against his hand and hated herself for loving the feel of it. He ran his finger over the shape of her ear, followed the line of her jaw, then moved lower, to the little pulse beating at her throat.

"I'm going to have to kiss you, Miss Porter," he whispered, bending close.

He saw the panic in her eyes and drew back. Thinking quickly, he decided to keep things light.

"You're a cruel woman, Alexandra Porter. And a cool one. Here I am, wearing my heart on my sleeve, and you won't even acknowledge that you've noticed."

"Funny. I thought that heart had Milly's name on it."

He smiled, deciding to play it her way. Keep it light. "Fickle heart. One minute it throbs for food, the next for plain old passion."

"A smart man would go for the food."

"Not a brain in my head," he muttered, brushing his lips over her forehead.

"A pity." She felt a tiny tremor begin to inch along her spine at his light touch. "Milly admires intelligence."

"And how about Alexandra Porter?" He moved his mouth over her temple, leaving light, feathery kisses on her skin.

"She prefers them dumb," she whispered. "Dumb but virile." Her hand clutched his waist.

"My kind of woman. I fit the bill perfectly." His lips roamed her face, lightly touching the corners of her eyes, the tip of her nose, the slope of her jaw.

"I'm all wrong for you. You accused me of being cold and cruel."

"Is that what I said?" He felt her fingers tighten at his waist, and thrilled to her response. "Want to know what I think now?" He brushed his lips over hers, then lifted his head.

With a feeling of regret, her lids fluttered, then opened wide. "What?"

"I think you're a terrible liar." He caught her lower lip between his teeth, nipping lightly.

"And I think you'd better stop this."

"It could lead to a real, honest-to-goodness kiss." He brushed his lips gently over hers.

Desire washed over her in a rush of heat, and she pulled back, staring at him with a stricken look. How could one man make her so angry and then so joyous? And how could he make her forget all her good intentions so easily?

As he continued to hold her, the heat spread, bringing a flush to her skin, leaving her weak. Her grip on his waist tightened, and her fingertips found the gap where his shirt had pulled away from his waistband. His skin was warm and firm and inviting.

She felt him catch his breath at her touch. "Witch," he whispered against her ear. His warm breath feathered across her cheek.

Footsteps alerted them that someone was coming. They stiffened.

"Are we going?"

At the sound of the childish voice in the doorway, they both looked up. Immediately Alexandra took a step backward. It took her several seconds to unscramble her thoughts. She took a deep breath before replying. "I think I've been outvoted. Looks like we're going to the cider mill."

When Charley had finished shrieking her enthusiasm, Alexandra added, "Tell Milly she's included in the plans."

The little girl vanished, then reappeared almost instantly. "Milly says she wouldn't miss it."

"Neither would I. Unless, of course, I had an attic to clean." At Clif's lazy drawl, Alexandra gave him a quick, searching glance before turning away.

Her voice was steady again. "I think the next person who drops by uninvited will be handed a pail and bucket and sent to the top floor."

"Maybe the uninvited guest wouldn't complain, if he had someone . . . interesting to work with."

"I'll remember that," she flung over her shoulder. "Milly would love your company."

Clif lounged in the doorway and watched as mother and daughter climbed the stairs. This hadn't been at all what he'd expected. The dedicated career woman was a mother, raising a child alone. And she was absolutely terrified of getting involved. The amazing Miss Porter just continued to surprise him. How many more tricks were in her bag? he wondered, shaking a cigarette from a pack.

Chapter Six

The cider mill was a two-story building of weathered red clapboard perched on the side of a swollen creek. On the hills surrounding it were acres of apple orchards. In the autumn sunshine, the countryside was a blaze of color.

Clif parked the car in a small roped-off area. With Charley running ahead, tugging impatiently on Milly's arm, they walked toward the mill.

"Does she ever walk?" Clif asked.

"Not if she can run." Alexandra laughed. "I shudder to think what would happen if she could fly."

"She's delightful."

Alexandra wrinkled her nose. "I agree. Of course, I'm prejudiced. But I do think she talks too much."

"Unlike her mother, who is extremely closemouthed." He dropped a hand beneath her elbow. "Afraid of what she'll say?"

Alexandra paused, ordering herself to show no emotion at his touch. Afraid? Or merely cautious? Once burned . . .

"Hurry up, you two," Charley called from the wide porch.

Clif stopped to pluck a ruby oak leaf from a tree. Tucking it behind Alexandra's ear, he stood back, admiring. "With that coloring, your parents should have named you 'Autumn.' It suits you."

She stiffened. "All those sweet words just roll off your tongue like melted butter. Did you rehearse them before you came?"

He grinned at her icy tone. "Not very trusting, are you?" At her quick frown, he caught her hand. "Charley's getting impatient."

Dry leaves crunched beneath their feet. As they drew nearer the mill, the sharp tang of apples teased their senses. Clif pulled open a massive wooden door. A bell sounded their arrival. Inside, the aroma was stronger, even more tantalizing.

A tall, spare woman approached. Dressed in a long, old-fashioned gingham dress and spotless apron, her iron-gray hair tucked under a starched white cap, she looked like a figure from a history book.

At the eager expression on Charley's face, she broke into a smile.

Extending her hand, she said, "I'm Priscilla Barrow. Everyone calls me Prissy."

As usual, the little bundle of energy took over. "My name's Charley Porter." The little girl shook her hand solemnly, then turned. "This is my mom, and my friend, Milly. And this is my new friend, Clif Andrews."

Alexandra saw the smile of pleasure that lit Clif's features at Charley's casually spoken words.

"Welcome to the old Barrow Mill," Prissy said. "This mill and the orchard beyond have been in our family for five generations. We still make our cider the way great-great-grandfather Barrow did. Would you like me to explain the process as we go?"

At their eager nods, the woman led them on a brisk walk to the rear of the barnlike building.

"It actually begins out there," she said, pointing to the fields beyond. "The apples are picked in our orchard and transported up the hill by truck." She gave Charley a quick smile. "Of course, in the beginning they were hauled by horse-drawn wagons. But we've managed to keep up with the times and still remain true to our heritage."

"Sounds like an excerpt from our Andrews Motors speeches," Clif whispered.

Alexandra shot Clif a look. "Pay attention. There's a quiz when this is over."

"I was never very good at tests."

"I'll remember that if you decide to surprise me with some sort of executive test," she said with a laugh.

"If I decide to surprise you, it won't be with a test." His words, though spoken softly, had an edge to them.

Alexandra found herself distracted by his nearness. She had convinced herself that a simple trip to a cider mill would be harmless. There was nothing harmless, she realized, about Clif Andrews. His was an overpowering personality.

Raising her voice above the continuous din, their tour guide showed them thousands of apples being washed and dumped whole into a hopper, then fed into a grinder where they were turned into mash.

"That mash has skins, pulp, seeds and stems in it. The whole apple," Prissy said proudly.

Stopping beside the ancient press, Prissy explained, "The mash is spread onto a series of nylon cloths that are stacked under this press. Then, with power generated by the stream outside, the press is slowly cranked down on the stack like this."

While they watched with mouths open, the giant press began slowly descending. The creaking old press was stained dark from a century of use. As the mash was crushed, raw cider rushed out and ran through filters.

"Those filters are necessary to catch any stray seeds or solids that slipped through the nylon cloth," Prissy explained. "As you can see, the entire process from beginning to end only takes about twenty minutes."

"You mean that's all there is?" Charley asked in surprise. "Is that real cider?"

"It's real," Prissy said proudly. "It's all natural. We use no preservatives. Of course," she cautioned, "because it's natural, it must be refrigerated. If we were to leave it at room temperature for a week, it would begin to ferment, or turn 'hard.'"

"Like a rock?" Charley asked innocently.

"No, 'hard' means it is slightly alcoholic," Prissy explained. "If we were to leave it even longer than a week, it would become cider vinegar." Taking Charley's hand, she said, "I'll bet you'd like a sample of this freshly made cider, wouldn't you?"

"You bet."

Prissy lifted a dipper of the amber liquid from the vat and poured it into paper cups.

Sipping slowly, they sighed their appreciation. "Wonderful," Milly said, holding out her cup for another taste.

"In our country kitchen we sell cider, doughnuts and assorted apple jams and jellies."

As Milly and Charley followed the old woman toward the bright calico-trimmed kitchen, Clif caught Alexandra's arm.

"Let them browse a minute."

"And what will we do?"

He patted an old wooden bench. "We'll just sit here and breathe in the wonderful smells of this old mill."

Still sipping the cider, she sat down beside him.

"Sorry I bullied you into this?" he asked.

Her eyes were wary. "I still don't care for your heavy-handed tactics. But I'm awfully glad I came along. Can you believe this is my first trip to a mill?"

"This one's been here since 1900, and you never found time to visit. I can see we're going to have to do something about your free time, Miss Porter. Life is too short to spend it all climbing corporate ladders. Some of it should be spent lying under the shade of an old apple tree."

"Tell that to my boss," she said with a chuckle.

"Your boss has been working you much too hard," he said, staring deeply into her eyes.

Feeling a blush stain her cheeks, Alexandra turned away.

"I can see that I'm going to have to take you in hand." Clif's tone caught her attention, causing her to turn back to him. Without warning, he caught her arm and drew her close, brushing her lips with his. She froze, then drew away quickly. With a smile, he ran his tongue over his lips, savoring the apple flavor that lingered there.

"A bit tart for my taste," he murmured, "but I'll bet we can sweeten it up."

Alexandra stood so quickly that some of the cider sloshed over the rim of her cup. "Save the sweets for someone who'll appreciate them. I get the feeling that everything you say has been said before—to other, more gullible women."

She wasn't expecting the hand that snaked out and caught her wrist, holding her firmly in place. "You're afraid to believe anything good about me." His tone hardened. "Why?"

She stared down at his hand, then up at his cool, metallic-looking eyes. "Why should I?"

He stood, still holding her firmly. She could feel the power in his grip.

"Who hurt you, Alex?" It was a man, he knew instinctively. And even without knowing a thing about him, he hated him.

He saw the look that came and went in her eyes. "Don't call me 'Alex.' My name is Alexandra. And my life is none of your business."

"Oh, lady, I intend to make it my business," he said fiercely as she yanked her hand free.

She turned away. "Charley and Milly will be wondering what's happened to us."

"Come on, then." He dismissed the emotions churning inside him and caught her hand. "Let's have some more of that wonderful cider."

Charley came bounding toward them. "Prissy says we can take our cider and doughnuts out to the orchard. She says there are picnic tables and trails out there. We can even pick the apples if we find any left on the trees."

Clif bought a jug of fresh cider and half a dozen doughnuts, still warm from the oven. Under the shade of a gnarled apple tree, they sat at a weathered picnic table and lazily enjoyed their fare as if it were a feast.

"Let's take this trail and see if we can find any apples to pick," Clif suggested.

When they came to a low branch, Clif lifted Charley in his arms while she plucked two red apples.

"One for you, and one for me," she said, offering him the bigger one.

"Now we need two more." He led her to a second tree and again lifted her high on his shoulders so that she could reach two more apples.

Their little group walked slowly back along the trail, polishing apples on their sleeves and sinking their teeth into the crunchy fruit.

* * *

By the time they headed for home, the dusk of evening was settling across the countryside. Charley's nose was pressed to the window as she stared at the headlights of the cars they passed. Her eyes were growing heavy.

To keep her mind off the man beside her, Alexandra forced herself to concentrate on the conversation between Milly and Clif.

"You actually danced on Broadway?"

"Only for a year." Milly's voice became animated. "I was the stand-in for the star of the Follies for six months, and I'd begun to think my break would never come. Then one night the star ran off with a violinist from the orchestra. The director shoved me onstage and said, 'Kid, we're depending on you.'" Milly gave a chuckle of pure delight. "The next thing I knew, I had my name in lights."

"That's wonderful. Why only a year?" Clif expertly turned the car from the dirt road onto the highway.

"My real love was the ballet. When I was only ten years old, I danced in the *Nutcracker*. From that point on, there was never anything else I wanted to do. So when the Broadway show folded, I went back to the ballet corps in New York."

"Did you ever get to dance the lead?"

Milly's voice lowered. "That was my dream. It took me so many years to get to the top. Finally I was offered the lead in *Romeo and Juliet*."

Clif's tone showed his admiration. "You must have been so proud to dance that part."

"I never danced it." Milly's voice had a faraway tone.

"Why?"

"I met Ben." There was a smile in her voice. "And suddenly nothing else mattered. Not even dancing the lead in *Romeo and Juliet*."

"You don't sound sorry about your decision."

"Sorry?" Milly laughed. "That man made me feel like the most important woman in the whole world."

Clif glanced at Alexandra's profile in the darkness. "You're a lucky lady, Milly. Not everyone finds a great love in his or her life."

"I know." The older woman dropped an arm around the sleepy child beside her. "I wish everyone could be as happy as Ben and I were."

Alexandra kept her face averted and felt the sting of tears. Love. It was such a dangerous emotion. Ambitious people were willing to gamble all they'd worked for, their very futures, for that elusive thing. And often, when they thought they had it all, they discovered they'd thrown it all away for empty promises. They were left with nothing but pain and bitterness.

"Any regrets?" Clif asked.

"Not one," Milly responded.

Alexandra turned to glance at the man beside her. She'd discovered facets of him today that were completely unexpected. Although she still resented his intrusion into her private life, the day had been fun, not only for Charley and Milly, but for her, as well. It was obvious that her daughter adored his attentions. Milly was able to talk to him like an old friend. In fact, Alexandra thought, she'd never heard Milly open up about her past life with anyone else the way she had just now with Clif.

When Clif turned off the ignition, she was startled to find they were home.

"You'll come in for coffee, won't you, Clif?" Milly asked.

He was about to refuse when he caught sight of Alexandra's little frown of annoyance.

He swallowed a laugh. "I'd like that."

Stifling a yawn, Charley opened the back door. "I wish I was little again, so you'd carry me, Mom."

"Yesterday you were wishing you were old enough to wear lipstick."

"But I'm tired."

Clif grinned. "Come on, Charley. Climb on my back. I'll give you a ride to the house."

With a smile of triumph, the little girl wrapped her arms around his neck and giggled as he hauled her across the front porch.

"Make yourself comfortable," Milly said to Clif as Alexandra led Charley upstairs.

Trailing Milly to the kitchen, Clif leaned his hip against the doorway and watched as she filled the coffeepot.

"How old is Charley?" Clif asked absently.

"Eight. Isn't she something?" Milly opened the refrigerator and brought out a plate of biscuits.

"Yeah. Something." Clif was silent a moment. From the personnel records, he knew that Alexandra was twenty-six. That meant that she'd been only eighteen when Charley was born. Eighteen. Barely more than a child herself.

"How long have you known Alexandra?" Clif asked casually.

"Let's see." Milly set the table as she spoke. "Ben and I bought the house seven years ago. We used to watch Alexandra dash off to classes with that little baby strapped to her back." Milly's voice grew dreamy. "Ben and I always wanted a baby." She shrugged. "It wasn't meant to be. But when I lost Ben, I just needed to fill my life with someone—or something." She straightened and gave him a big smile. "And there were those two special people needing someone who had a little time on her hands. We're all good for each other."

Alexandra sailed down the stairs and paused in the doorway. Feeling Clif's intense gaze, she moved past him and began folding napkins. She needed to stay busy to hide her nervousness.

"Poor Charley. She could barely keep her eyes open long enough to undress. She was asleep the minute her head hit the pillow."

"The coffee's ready," Milly said, pouring two cups.

"You aren't staying?" A look of panic darted into Alexandra's eyes.

"Can't. All that walking did me in. I'm going home to soak in a warm tub."

"Stay awhile, Milly." Alexandra had to force herself to keep a pleading note out of her voice.

Clif watched her in silence. She was scared to death. Of what?

Dropping a hand on her shoulder, Milly said cheerfully, "I'll see you in the morning. Clif." Milly turned and offered her hand. "This was fun. I hope I see you again."

"You can count on it. Good night, Millicent."

When the door closed behind her, Alexandra lifted the two cups and placed them on the table.

"Cream or sugar?"

"Black."

He sat and watched as she continued to move around the kitchen.

"Did you bake these?"

She turned. "Milly and Charley made them. I don't bake."

He buttered a biscuit and bit into it. "Wonderful. Want one?"

She shook her head and took a seat across from him.

"What other things don't you do?" he asked softly.

Her eyes widened as she stared at him. "What do you mean?"

"You don't bake. You don't say much. You don't let anyone get close to you. What else don't you do?"

Her tone hardened. "I don't tolerate intrusions into my personal life. And I don't answer impertinent questions."

"Why the fence, Alex?"

He saw her stiffen.

"You've erected a fence and hung out a No Trespassing sign."

"Then I'd appreciate it if you would respect my wishes."

He drained his coffee and stood. For the first time his voice lost its teasing note. "All right. Sorry for the inconvenience. The truth is, I had a great time."

As he strode to the front door, she took a deep breath and followed him.

"Clif."

He turned, his hand on the knob.

"Please excuse my manners." She sighed and spoke the rest of the words in a rush. "Charley and Milly had a wonderful time today. Thank you."

"And you?"

He saw her bite her lip before responding softly, "I enjoyed myself." She stared at a spot on the floor.

Leaning his back against the door, he folded his arms across his chest. "There. That didn't hurt, did it?"

Her eyelids fluttered. She glanced up in time to see a slight smile appear on his lips. As he took a step closer, the fear leaped back into her eyes.

He extended his hand. "I was simply going to suggest a friendly handshake."

She let out a shaky breath. With a weak smile she offered her hand. It was engulfed in his.

"Good night, Miss Porter."

"Good night, Mr. Andrews."

He thought about taking her into his arms and crushing her lips with his. He thought about how it would feel to have her soft body pressed against his. Recalling their unfinished kiss and her surprisingly sweet surrender, he realized how easy it would be to take what he wanted. Then, remembering the fear in her eyes that must have been caused by great pain, he banked his own needs. What she needed was to trust again. If he was patient, if he took his time, he could earn that trust.

He held her hand a moment longer. He wasn't a patient man. But he was a man who knew what he wanted and how to get it. If it was patience the lady needed, he'd have it in abundance.

With a last glance at her flushed cheeks, he turned and pulled the door open. As he climbed into his car, she was still standing in the doorway, silhouetted in the lamplight. Even from this distance, she appeared small, fragile, vulnerable.

Chapter Seven

I think you'll be interested in this little item," Marion said, thrusting a newspaper in front of her nephew.

Clif read quickly, then glanced up at her.

"Where did you get this?"

"Frank Tuller. He picked it up in New York yesterday."

"Why didn't he come to me? He knows I'm conducting an investigation into these leaks."

"Maybe Frank agrees with me that you're being too... soft on this issue."

"Soft?" His voice deepened with controlled anger. "Do you really think I'd take a thing like this lightly?"

"I think you may be getting too... emotionally involved to be objective."

Clif sat back in his chair, assessing his aunt. "Say what you mean, Marion."

"Frank took his grandson to an old cider mill last Saturday. He said he could have sworn he passed you and the new manager of Division Two, Miss Porter, driving away."

Clif stood, scraping back his chair. "My private life is just that, Marion. Private. What I choose to do away from the office is my business."

"Not if it colors your judgment," she said quickly.

He spoke quietly, trying to swallow back the seething anger he felt. His hands gripped the edge of his desk until the knuckles were white from the effort. "When it comes to this company, I can be as ruthless as anyone. Believe me, Marion, my...friendship with an employee will never come before the good of our shareholders."

She gave him a frigid smile. "How reassuring. Then I can assume you will ask your...friend, Miss Porter, for her resignation?"

"If and when she is proven guilty."

"I have your word on that?"

The words came out in a hiss. "You have my word on it."

He felt a rush of impotent fury as his aunt gave him a smug look before striding from his office.

Clif sat down heavily and reread the newspaper article. Then, staring into space, he thought about his aunt, a major stockholder, and Frank Tuller, who had been her friend for over thirty years. Once there had been rumors of a romance between them, but they had gone their separate ways. Still, they voted together on every issue. And now Frank had chosen to go to Marion instead of to him. Clif tapped a pen against his desk top. He couldn't afford to lose an important ally...to a woman who would go to any length to get what she wanted.

The week passed in a blur of phone messages, paperwork and meetings. Alexandra discovered that the position of division manager required even more of her time than she'd expected. There were confidential test results to study, interoffice memos to be dictated, and even personnel conflicts to be mediated. Though she was beginning to feel the strain, she was determined to handle the responsibility in a professional manner.

The article in the magazine she'd found on her assistant's desk weighed heavily on her mind. On Friday, she asked him to come into her office.

"Mike, close the door please."

Puzzled, he crossed the room and closed the door, shutting out the office sounds beyond.

"What's up, Alexandra?"

She indicated the chair beside her desk. "We have to talk about something."

He sat quickly.

"I spotted a copy of this month's *Wheels Magazine* on your desk. I hope you don't mind, but I leafed through it."

He shrugged. "You know it's there for anyone who wants to read it." He waited, visibly tense.

"There was a report on our confidential testing of new paints and finishes. It was accurate down to the last detail."

Mike made a steeple of his hands and stared over them. "I saw it."

"It had to come from this department."

He nodded. "I agree."

She paused. "Why didn't you point it out to me?"

Clear blue eyes met hers. "I didn't want to worry you."

"Worry me?" She stood and paced in agitation. Whirling, she said, "My neck is on the chopping block, and you don't want me to worry?"

He stood, towering over her. "I was hoping I could find out where the leak came from before I told you about it."

Her voice deepened with emotion. "This is my division, Mike. I have the right to know everything that goes on here. And you had a duty to come to me with this information as soon as you learned of it."

"I'm sorry." He passed a hand over his brow. He was sweating profusely, she noted. "When I first read it, I suspected Bill Campbell. There'd been a glaring error in one of his reports. I thought it might have been made deliberately." He met her narrow look. "To test us. To see if we were paying attention."

"And now?"

He shook his head. "I've been looking over his shoulder ever since. I can't find anything suspicious. I'm beginning to think the leak came from someone else."

Her next words were spoken with that cool, precise delivery he knew so well. "Your first mistake was not coming to me immediately. Your second was picking a fight with Bill Campbell in front of everyone at the division meeting. Even if he did leak those test results, he'll be very careful until he thinks you've given up on him."

"You mean you think he could be the one?"

"I mean," she said with venom, "that everyone in this division is suspect."

Mike assessed her for long, silent moments. "Even me?"

The phone on her desk shattered the strained silence. For a moment she ignored the ringing.

His voice lowered with emotion. "Am I a suspect, Alexandra?"

She gave a barely perceptible nod of her head. With quick, angry strides, Mike crossed the room and threw open the door. When it closed loudly behind him, she picked up the phone.

Impatiently, she snapped, "Alexandra Porter here."

"Miss Porter." The sound of Clif's deep voice had her nerves quivering. "I'd like to see you immediately in my office."

She swallowed. "I'll be there in ten minutes."

"Make it five."

She stared at the phone as the line went dead.

Ignoring the pile of paperwork on her desk, she walked to the elevator and rode to the executive offices.

"Good afternoon, Miss Porter," Martha James called in her perpetually cheerful voice. "Go right in. Mr. Andrews is expecting you."

"Thank you."

She strode through the doorway and heard his secretary close the double doors behind her.

Although Clif was talking on the phone with his back to the door, he knew the moment she entered. As she crossed the room, he swiveled his chair and continued talking while his gaze followed her movements. Her very walk left him weak. He frowned.

"Thanks, Phil. I'll get back to you." Without glancing away from her, he replaced the receiver.

"You wanted to see me?"

"Yes." Desperately, he realized. There had been no time to see her all week. They'd been on separate treadmills, running as quickly as they could, but getting no closer to each other. Now that she was here, his aunt's suspicions seemed ridiculous.

To keep from reaching out to her, he picked up a pencil and tapped it against the desk top. "Has anyone in your department been giving you trouble?"

She thought about the scene with Mike and flushed. "Everyone's doing his job."

"I'm interested in disgruntled employees. Any complaints lately about the long hours of testing? A salary dispute maybe?"

She tensed. Did he suspect something, or was he just fishing? She could tell him of her suspicions. But she would be reacting like a weak-willed woman unsure of her new position. She would rather get to the bottom of this problem herself and then bring it to his attention. She shook her head. "I'm not aware of anyone who's unhappy."

He lifted the pencil and held it between the thumb and finger of each hand, rotating it slowly. "How are you handling the pressures of division management?"

She folded her hands primly in her lap. "Just fine."

"Then there are no problems?" Tell me, he pleaded silently. Tell me you know about the leaks. Tell me you have a suspicion.

"Nothing I can't handle."

"Has your assistant patched things up with Bill Campbell?"

"I don't believe they'll have any further problems."

He cleared his throat. "I've read the latest test results from Emmet's department."

She looked up to meet his probing gaze.

"They sound promising."

She swallowed. "We're happy with them. I think Emmet's close to a breakthrough."

"You realize how important it is that no one find out about these tests. If our competitors should get advance warning, they could beat us to the marketplace."

"We're all aware of the importance of secrecy." She had to look away. "Is there anything else?"

The pencil snapped in two. He tossed the fragments on his desk. "That's all."

She stood and began to cross the room.

He swore and rounded his desk. Catching her roughly by the arm, he twisted her around to face him.

"No. That isn't all. Something's wrong, Alexandra. What is it?"

"Nothing." She tried vainly to break free of his grasp.

"Are there problems in your department?"

She shook her head. She needed to prove to herself that she could handle these problems in a professional manner. "I have a lot on my mind. There are dozens of new responsibilities."

"Too much to handle?"

"Of course not, Mr. Andrews."

He heard the outrage in her tone and chided himself for his insensitivity. His voice lowered seductively. "Maybe this whole thing was just an excuse to see you. Let's go somewhere after work. Have a drink. Talk."

"I can't." She stared at a point beyond his shoulder.

With his thumb and finger he lifted her chin. "Can't? Or won't?"

His touch made her weak, a feeling she despised in herself. Expelling a long sigh, she met his eyes. "I can't afford to be seen with the president of the company. Everyone would talk."

"Let them."

"That's easy for you. Do you know what they would say? That I got my promotion by cozying up to the boss."

He swore. "I never even met you until the board approved your promotion."

"No one would ever believe that."

He stared down into those cool green eyes and felt a surge of desire that nearly took his breath away.

"Lady, you are the most practical, the most levelheaded, the most frustratingly uncooperative woman I've ever met. You're straining my patience to the limit."

"Really," she returned coolly. "I hadn't noticed that you had any patience to strain."

"You're right." Still holding her chin firmly, he bent his head and brushed his lips over hers. "I don't," he murmured against her mouth.

He saw a look of surprise leap into her eyes before she tried to push him away. He grasped her shoulders, drawing her roughly against him.

Alexandra stiffened, afraid to move, afraid even to breathe. His eyes pinned her. Those eyes that never revealed his thoughts now seemed transparent. In them she could read desire, a desire that matched her own. Hot, blazing passion flared between them. It was a passion so intense, so compelling that she felt her fear slowly turn to a kind of horrible fascination as she watched him sway toward her. One look from this man was enough to arouse her.

The hands at her shoulders tightened. "I told you I wasn't a patient man."

"Don't, Clif. I don't want..."

"You want, Alexandra Porter," he snarled. "You and I both want."

She stiffened, fighting to hold herself rigid in his arms. His mouth covered hers in a kiss that caused an explosion of feeling inside her. In that single moment everything changed. She felt both hot and cold, and oddly exhilarated.

He lifted his head and studied her from beneath hooded lids. She could see by the stunned expression on his face that he'd felt it, too.

He bent again to her lips. Her mouth was as soft as the underside of a rose petal. He moved his lips over hers, tasting her sweet, exotic flavor.

He'd felt the chemistry the first time he saw her. He'd expected the kiss to fire his blood, to unleash his passion. The rush of heat, the surge of desire were not unexpected. What he hadn't expected was this hunger, this need that bordered on pain. Taking the kiss deeper, he ran a hand along her back, feeling her delicate bones. If he wasn't careful, he'd crush her.

He changed the angle of the kiss and brought his hand beneath the jacket of her trim business suit. Silk. The blouse was silk. Like her skin. Like her hair. He yearned to explore the body that taunted him just beneath the silk. But her lips held him enthralled. He'd never tasted anything so sweet. He'd never felt himself wanting to give and take so desperately.

Her heartbeat thundered, sending a rush of heat through her veins. He wasn't at all what she'd expected. The hands at her shoulders were strong, so strong they could break her. His touch was fierce, almost driven. His kiss was demanding, draining her, taking more than she'd ever known she could give. The strength she sensed in him left her dazed and frightened.

She gave up the struggle to reason. She could no longer hold a single thought. The only thing she was aware of was the pleasure of the moment.

Her hands, which had balled into fists at his touch, now opened and curled into the front of his shirt, drawing him closer. Though she hadn't wanted this, she responded with a hunger that matched his own. Desire was swift, catching her by surprise. Her tongue met his, then entered his mouth. His moan made her pulse hammer in her temples. She lost track of time and place. There was only this man, this kiss and the pleasure his lips brought her.

A knock on the door startled both of them.

"Mr. Andrews, Frank Tuller is here to see you."

With a moan, Clif buried his face in her hair and struggled to gather his thoughts. Her taste, her scent were too overpowering. He had nearly taken her, here in his sterile office, with hundreds of employees just beyond the door. What sort of madness gripped him?

Lifting his head, Clif continued holding Alexandra firmly against him. He could feel her taking in deep gulps of air to steady her ragged breathing. Her body still trembled at his touch.

He swore in frustration and ran a hand through his hair. He needed to think clearly but it was impossible with this woman in his arms. He had ordered Tuller to drop everything and report to the executive office.

"Tell Frank to take a seat, Martha. I'll see him in a minute."

As her footsteps receded, he took a step backward, all the while watching Alexandra. Her lips were still warm and moist from his kiss. Her cheeks were flushed, her eyes still dark with desire. With a single touch that desire could be coaxed into flame once more. The thought made him clench his fists at his sides.

Running a hand nervously over her hair, she turned and reached for the door.

His cool tone stopped her. "I still want to see you later."

She kept her back to him. "I'm afraid not. This doesn't change a thing." She took a deep breath and squared her shoulders. She pulled the door open and strode past his secretary and the man who sat waiting in the outer office without seeing them.

Oh, but it changes everything, Miss Porter, Clif thought with a frown. Behind the prim facade, passion slumbered. He'd had a sample. Now he wanted to taste it all.

"I can't believe I let you talk me into this." Alexandra scowled at her daughter's reflection beside her in the mirror.

"Clif said he'll do all the cooking. All you have to do is eat."

"Thanks a lot. You make me sound like a human garbage disposal. Do you think I'm helpless?"

"Only in the kitchen. Can you fix this ponytail?"

Alexandra tugged on her daughter's hair. "This is the last time I'm going to allow you to take my phone calls. What I'd like to know is how Clif Andrews found out that Milly was going out of town this weekend."

"I told him." At her mother's sudden frown, Charley added, "I told him you were in the shower. Then he asked me if we'd had dinner yet. And I told him we'd probably make grilled-cheese sandwiches." She wrinkled her nose. "Your specialty. And that's when he invited us over."

"And you accepted his invitation without first checking with me. What if I'd already made other plans?"

"You never make plans without me for the weekend, Mom."

The words were spoken so simply that Alexandra paused to study her daughter. It was true. She couldn't remember the last time she'd made any weekend plans that didn't include Charley.

"Come on, Mom. Clif said he was going to start the grill right away." She turned. "Oh. And he said to bring a bathing suit."

"In this weather?" Alexandra gazed at the dreary rain pelting the windows.

"That's what he said."

"You can bring your suit if you want," her mother said. "I prefer warm slacks and an even warmer sweater."

Charley rummaged in her drawer and stuffed her bathing suit into the pocket of her sweatshirt. "Just in case," she said, seeing her mother's raised eyebrow.

Alexandra drove slowly, hoping to put off the meeting with Clif for as long as possible. Just thinking about the scene in his office made her cheeks redden. He was a dangerous man. She would have to go to even greater lengths to keep her distance from him.

So she was taking her daughter to dinner at his house. That was a great way to keep her distance, she thought with self-disgust. This was the last time she would allow herself to be manipulated by the two of them.

Driving slowly along the curving Lakeshore Drive, she had no trouble finding the Andrews estate. The house, a lovely, sprawling three-story building of English Tudor design, had weathered three generations gracefully. The gardens were carefully manicured, showing off a profusion of brilliant mums. The trees, cloaked in autumn fire, added to the display. A circular drive led to wide front steps lined with pots of bright late-blooming flowers.

"Ooh. Is this Clif's house, Mom?"

Alexandra nodded and fought down the fluttering in her stomach. She was no stranger to her boss's lifestyle. She had turned her back on it years ago.

Charley was out of the car and running up the steps before her mother had the key out of the ignition. Following slowly, Alexandra smiled at the formally dressed man who opened the door.

"Mr. Andrews is expecting you, ladies. My name is Burtan. I'll show you the way."

"Hi, Burtan." Charley offered her hand. While Alexandra stifled a laugh, the man arched his eyebrows and stiffly accepted the outstretched hand. "My name's Charley Porter. This is my mother, Alexandra."

"Miss Porter." He looked up. "Mrs. Porter. Follow me, please."

A Georgian table in the entrance hall displayed a cluster of Fu dogs. Above it hung an eighteenth-century French screen decorated with scenes from *Aesop's Fables*. As they walked along a wide gallery that ran the length of the house, Alexandra had a glimpse of a formal living room and a wood-paneled library, its walls lined with leather-bound volumes.

The kitchen was at the back of the house. A floor of gleaming black-and-white tiles and walls and cabinets of pristine white gave an impression of space. Over an island counter, pots, pans and utensils hung in casual disarray. Standing at the sink, dressed in faded denims, the sleeves of his shirt rolled above his elbows, was Clif.

As they paused in the doorway, a bundle of fur hurtled toward them, giving a series of loud barks. Seeing Charley, the pup threw himself into her arms, then stood on its hind legs to lick her face.

"Ooh, Mom. A puppy. Isn't he beautiful?"

"And friendly, from the way he's slobbering all over you."

Clif quickly dried his hands and hurried toward them.

"This is MacLaren," he said, smiling at the frisky puppy covering Charley's face with kisses.

"He's beautiful," Charley said with a sigh. "What kind of dog is he, Clif?"

"A Sheltie. That's a Shetland Sheepdog. They've been bred in Scotland for generations. They're loyal and hard-working and most of all friendly, as you can see."

"Oh, MacLaren," Charley said, throwing her arms around his neck, "you're going to lick me to death."

"They're also a little unruly. Especially if they've been abandoned shortly after birth."

"Oh, how awful." Alexandra bent to the dog. "Who could do such a thing?"

"Someone who didn't want to bother with a litter of pups, obviously."

Turning to his elderly houseman, Clif touched his shoulder. "Thank you, Burtan. I won't need you any longer tonight."

The man nodded stiffly. "Good night, Mr. Andrews. Ladies."

"Night, Burtan," Charley called. Looking around, she said, "This kitchen's as big as our whole house. I'd never get all those pots and pans washed."

Clif laughed. "Neither would I. That's why I have someone do them for me."

"You mean you don't have to take turns doing the dishes?"

Clif laughed. As he turned to Alexandra, his smile deepened. "I'm glad you were able to come."

"Charley didn't leave me much choice. You're very good at this, aren't you?"

"What?" he asked innocently.

"Making plans with my daughter, then acting as though I'm a villain if I don't go along."

He smiled. "Is that what I do?"

She shot him a knowing look. "Try that innocent act on someone else, Mr. Andrews." She glanced around. "Who's doing the cooking?"

"I am." Seeing her surprised expression, he said, "Cooking relaxes me. Whenever I have time on the weekends, I prefer to make my own meals. This evening I've sent the help home."

"We're alone?"

He took a step closer, inhaling her delicate scent. "All alone," he said conspiratorially. "Just you and me. And Charley and MacLaren," he added, turning to the child who was exploring the kitchen with the puppy at her heels. "Did you bring your bathing suit?"

The little girl bounded across the room. "I did. But Mom said it's too cold to go swimming."

"Not in my pool." Catching Charley's hand, he said, "Come on. I'll show you. In this house, we can swim all year long."

At the doorway he turned to Alexandra. "Coming?"

She caught up with them and forced herself to smile. Even if the help had all gone for the night, she wasn't completely alone with Clif. There was Charley.

Relax, she reminded herself. What could possibly happen in the company of her daughter?

Clif touched her hand, sending little tremors skittering along her spine. She glanced up in time to see the light dancing in his eyes. Anything, her mind responded. When it came to Clif Andrews, anything was possible. He had a way of making things happen.

Chapter Eight

The southern side of the house had been transformed into a solarium. Three walls of glass looked out onto formal gardens. In the daytime skylights would offer even more light. In the center of the room a graceful free-form pool shimmered invitingly. Trees and rose bushes in containers were arranged around the pool, as well as a profusion of potted plants. Despite the faint lingering aroma of chlorine, the room smelled like a summer garden.

"Oh, Clif, this is beautiful."

He was oddly pleased by Alexandra's reaction. "I had this added a few years ago," he said. "With Michigan's short summer, it seemed more practical to have a pool indoors. I like daily physical exercise."

It showed, she thought, noting the muscles in his arms, and his trim, flat stomach.

"Can I swim in it?" Charley asked excitedly.

"That's what it's here for," Clif remarked. "You can change in that room." He turned to Alexandra. "Care to join us?"

Seeing the lovely setting, she regretted not having a bathing suit. "Sorry. I'll have to settle for watching."

"I'll be back in a minute."

As Clif walked away, Alexandra began slowly circling the room, touching the blooms of a peach-colored rose, bending to inhale the wonderful fragrance of a gardenia plant. When he returned, he was carrying a tray that he set on a glass-topped wicker table.

"I thought you might enjoy some wine while you watch," he said, handing her a long-stemmed glass.

Charley came strolling out in her bathing suit, tested the water with her toe, then hugged her knees to her chest and tumbled into the pool.

"I forgot to ask," Clif said abruptly. "Can she swim?"

For the first time, Alexandra laughed. "It's a little late to be asking that. But just to ease your mind, she's an excellent swimmer."

He let out a sigh. "I'm not used to little girls jumping in my pool."

"Only big ones?" She set the glass down and turned to him with a smug look.

At her sideways glance, he threw back his head and roared. "Careful, Miss Porter, or I may be tempted to throw one big girl in."

"You wouldn't dare."

Her eyes widened as he scooped her up and carried her to the edge of the pool.

"Never issue a challenge to an Andrews, Miss Porter. We've never been known to refuse a dare."

"Clif." In her surprise she forgot to be formal. Wrapping her arms around his neck, she clung fiercely. "Don't. I didn't bring a change of clothes."

He liked having this independent woman clutching him so tightly. "I bet you'd look wonderful in a sheet." Clif glanced across the pool at Charley. "What do you say? Should I throw your mother in the pool, or spare her?"

Charley giggled and clapped her hands. "Oh, Mom, you should see your face."

Alexandra attempted her most intimidating tone of voice. "I'm warning both of you. I don't want to swim. This isn't funny."

"Getting a little hot under the collar, Miss Porter?"

"Mr. Andrews." She gritted her teeth as he stood poised at the edge of the pool. "Put me down."

"Anything you say, Miss Porter." With a roar of laughter, he dropped her into the water.

She came up sputtering. Her water-logged sweater billowed with water, then, like a balloon with the air suddenly released, drooped down around her hips, clinging to her like a second skin. She shook her head so that her hair danced around her, then floated on the surface of the water. Wiping the moisture from her eyes, she swam to the side of the pool. Above her, Clif stood, legs apart, laughing hysterically.

Catching his ankle, she tugged with all her strength. For a moment he seemed to hang suspended above the water. Then with an enormous splash, he landed beside her in the pool. He came up with a look of astonishment and made a grab for her. Twisting free, she ducked behind him and pushed his head underwater.

"You landed like a big, fat hippopotamus," she said, clearly enjoying his punishment.

"You're in big trouble, lady," he called as he caught her shoulder.

Though she tried to evade him, he hauled her closer until she was pinned firmly against his hard, muscled body. Beneath the water, her breasts were flattened against his chest. Her thighs pressed against his. Her breathing was uneven from the exertion.

He tangled his legs around hers and began drawing her under the water. Holding her breath, she held him tightly, dragging his head under with her.

He gave her an admiring look as they surfaced. "You fight dirty."

"Only when I'm forced to," she muttered.

"You'll have to pay for that."

"I don't see what more you can do, now that you've practically drowned me," she fumed.

"I'll think of something." He ran a hand along her side and felt her trembling response to his touch.

"These heavy clothes are going to drag me under."

"You could take them off." She heard the warmth of laughter beneath the teasing words.

"You'd like that, wouldn't you?"

"Very much, Miss Porter. Care to oblige me?"

"Not on your life." She glanced across the pool to her daughter, who was still giggling at their antics. "While you two have a good time in the pool, I'm going to search for something dry to put on."

"There are robes in the changing room," Clif said, reluctantly letting her go. "Oh, no." He kicked his foot, sending up a spray of water. "You just ruined a new pair of shoes." He tried to sound angry as she pulled herself from the pool.

"Serves you right. I doubt this sweater will ever be the same." She glanced down in embarrassment at the shell-pink wool clinging to her torso. She might as well have been naked.

"I don't think I've ever seen you looking quite that good in a sweater before, Miss Porter," he called as she disappeared around the corner.

Nonchalantly he pulled himself up and sat on the edge of the pool. "There's just you and me now, Charley. Want to see my swan dive?"

"Sure."

Clinging to the edge of the pool, the little girl watched as Clif walked to the diving board. With streams of water dripping from his clothes, he gracefully spread his arms, then executed an outrageous belly flop into the pool. At his slapstick humor she collapsed in a fit of giggles while he swam the length of the pool and back.

"Aren't those wet clothes heavy?" she asked.

"Too heavy. They ruined my perfect dive. I think it's time to change."

He crossed the solarium to the changing room. Alexandra, dressed in a white terry robe several sizes too big, was combing the tangles from her dripping hair.

"My first mermaid," he said, coming up behind her.

"This one has feet instead of fins."

"But such great feet," he murmured. Bringing his arms around her waist, he watched her in the mirror. It gave him a strange feeling to see her in his robe. "I'll pay for the sweater."

"It'll dry. I think it'll survive." She grinned at his reflection. "Sorry about your shoes."

"But not too sorry." He lifted her wet hair and put his lips to her neck.

Her smile faded. Her voice sounded oddly strained. "Don't you think you'd better get out of those wet clothes and into bathing trunks?"

"I knew it. You're dying to see my body."

She dropped the brush with a clatter. "I'd rather watch Charley swim."

He marveled at how regally she moved in a robe several sizes too large.

"Pity," he murmured, enjoying the way the rough terry fabric clung to her damp hips. "I was hoping you'd stay and watch me change."

"Please," she said with mock sarcasm. "I don't want to get sick before that lovely dinner you promised."

"You're a tough one, Miss Porter." He began unbuttoning his wet shirt. "As soon as I'm decent, I'll have a quick swim with your daughter and then see to your food."

She shot him a triumphant smile before turning away. "I hope that watch you're wearing is waterproof."

She missed the look on his face as he stared in dismay at the expensive gold watch gleaming dully on his wrist.

Alexandra was pleasantly surprised. Dinner was good. In fact, she admitted, it was wonderful. Clif had tossed a garden salad with his own blended dressing. He cooked perfect steaks on an indoor grill. With them, he served steaming baked potatoes topped with sour cream.

"Let's have our dessert in front of the fireplace," he urged, carrying a tray of fruit and warm chocolate fondue into the great room.

A crackling fire was burning in a great stone fireplace. Outside, rain lashed the windows. Inside, they were content to be dry and warm.

For dessert Charley nibbled chocolate-covered cherries and strawberries while Clif and Alexandra sipped a glass of dry red wine.

"That was really wonderful, Clif. I never expected you to be such a good cook."

"You mean I managed to surprise you?"

He'd been a surprise from the first moment she'd met him, she thought with sudden insight. He fit none of the molds.

Alexandra was still wearing his robe. Clif had changed into dark corduroy slacks and a gray cashmere sweater. Somehow he had arranged it so that the two of them were sharing a sofa on one side of the fireplace. On the other side, Charley, tucked beneath a mohair throw, had one arm around a tired MacLaren, who stared mesmerized at the flames.

"Do you live here all alone, Clif?" Charley asked in a drowsy tone.

"Uh-humm."

"Don't you get lonesome in this big old house?"

He smiled at the little girl as she fought sleep. Beside her MacLaren had already succumbed. "Sometimes."

"Do you have a mom and dad?"

He shook his head. "They died a couple of years ago."

"Any brothers or sisters?"

"Enough questions, Charley," Alexandra said.

"I don't mind." Clif leaned back, stretching his legs out lazily toward the heat of the fire. "No brothers or sisters, Charley. Just me."

"It's a good thing you have MacLaren," she said, snuggling down beside the puppy and closing her sleepy eyes.

For long moments Clif studied the little girl and the sleeping puppy. Then he seemed to stir himself. "Ready for some coffee?" Clif asked.

Alexandra nodded.

"I'll be right back."

While he was gone, Alexandra studied her surroundings. This room, like the kitchen and the solarium, suited the man who lived here. A high studio ceiling was supported by massive oak beams. Skylights and a bank of floor-to-ceiling windows along one wall gave a feeling of light and space. Despite the bleak autumn storm, the room was cozy and warm. The high-backed sofas they were sitting in were arranged on either side of a granite fireplace. The furniture was a comfortable mix of contemporary and traditional. On one wall was a lovely set of original Audubon prints of Michigan birds. The painting over the mantel was a Wyeth. Much of this house reflected his parents' and grandparents' tastes. But this room, she knew, was uniquely Clif's.

A man of many tastes and moods, Alexandra thought. But a man who seemed to cherish the simple pleasures of home and work. A man who could be content to be surrounded by a loving family.

Clif returned with a tray containing a silver coffee service. Alexandra poured and handed him a cup.

"I believe you take yours black," she said, before turning back to pour a second cup.

If he was surprised that she remembered how he liked his coffee, he said nothing. Leaning back, he studied her.

Her hair had dried into soft, loose waves that fell below her shoulders. In the firelight it was dark molten flame. As she bent, the robe parted, revealing the shadowed cleft between her breasts. He felt the familiar stirring. Without makeup her skin was pale and translucent, her complexion flawless.

She turned to him with a smile. "Your home is beautiful, Clif. Have you had to do much remodeling?"

"Quite a bit. These old mansions tend to have a lot of rooms that seem archaic today. I really didn't need a music room, or a ballroom. I preferred rooms that would relate to my own lifestyle." He grinned. "So the ballroom now houses an indoor pool. And the music room is now the great room."

Tucking her feet beneath her, she sipped her coffee. "Did you ever want to be anything besides the president of Andrews Motors?"

Clif leaned back, smiling. "When I was very young, I wanted to be a sculptor. My grandmother was an artist, and my grandfather was a...tinkerer. He was always looking for new ways to make old things work. He loved fooling with other people's junk. That's how he happened to build an engine that revolutionized the automobile industry."

"Is that how he started Andrews Motors?"

He nodded. "Gramps sold the patent for ten thousand dollars, a grand sum to him. Then another man went on to make a million dollars from his idea." His tone lowered. "My grandfather lived by an old axiom: never get mad; get even. So he took every penny he'd saved and bought a competitor's company. He surrounded himself with the best and the brightest in the industry. Within five years, the millionaire who had bought his patent was working for him. And Andrews Motors was an automotive giant."

"That's an amazing story." She glanced at the man who sat beside her, the angles of his face in sharp relief against the gleaming flames. "Still wish you were a sculptor?"

He shook his head. "From the time I was old enough to know who I was, I've wanted to run the company. Like my grandfather, I love tinkering. I think that with the best people in the industry working for me, we can solve any problem. I've always believed in the automobile."

"What about your father?" Alexandra asked softly.

"He and his sister grew up in an era of overnight successes and overnight failures. I'm sure that colored their outlook." His voice softened. "My father and my aunt learned to like their status. I've always thought Dad liked being the owner of the Wolverine Football Team more than he liked being the president of Andrews Motors. Marion was the one who always coveted that title."

She heard the slight edge to his tone. "When your father died, why didn't she step into the role of president?"

"She tried. There was a lot of pressure brought to bear on certain members of the board to name her president. But most of them realized that Marion's ambition clouds her vision at times. She would never have been able to delegate. And she'd never have been able to reward those who deserved it. Marion is the type who wants to have it all. All the power, all the glory."

Setting his cup down, he caught her hand and brought it to his lips. "Enough shoptalk. Tell me about Alexandra Porter."

"A boring story," she said with a laugh.

"Then bore me." He moved closer, still holding her hand. "Do you have any family besides Charley?"

"My father and mother live on the West Coast. There are an aunt and uncle and several cousins scattered across the country. We're . . . not close."

He heard the slight tremor in her voice and decided not to pursue the subject. "No brothers or sisters?"

She shook her head. "Like you, I'm an only child."

"It has its disadvantages, don't you think?"

She glanced down at the hand holding hers. "I've always thought it would be fun to have lots of brothers and sisters. I've always wanted to be part of a large family."

"I had a friend in college who invited me to his home for spring break one year." Clif's voice warmed. "There were eight of them. The boys handsome, the girls absolutely beautiful. They didn't really need anyone else to have fun. But they were so warm, so loving that they made a guest feel like family. I admired them. And," he added softly, "I always knew that that was the kind of love, the kind of enthusiasm for life that I wanted to have. I decided then and there that I would be surrounded by lots of children and grandchildren."

Alexandra laughed. "How old are you, Clif?"

"Thirty-one."

"You'd better get started soon. You have a long way to go." Her laughter deepened. "Have you found a woman willing to give you eight children?"

"Not yet. But I'm looking. The women who are intelligent enough to interest me are too concerned with their own careers to consider having a family."

"You mean you're looking for a girl just like the girl who married dear old dad?"

His eyes crinkled into laughter. "My mother hated her family responsibilities. She preferred tennis, bridge and afternoon cocktails at the club."

Without thinking, Alexandra murmured, "I know the type. You've just described my mother."

Clif arched an eyebrow. It wasn't much of an admission. But this was the first time Alexandra Porter had revealed anything at all about her personal life. It was a start. The first chink in that wall.

Glancing at her sleeping daughter, Alexandra said softly, "I'd better check the dryer and see if my clothes are ready."

"Relax," he said. "We haven't finished that wine yet."

"Another time. I'd better get Charley home."

Glancing at the girl and dog, Clif said, "That's the first time MacLaren hasn't whined in his sleep. He still misses the comfort of his mother."

"Now you know the secret. Let him fall asleep with your arm around him."

"Given a choice," he murmured, drawing her closer, "I'd rather fall asleep with my arms around you." He pressed his lips to her temple.

Instantly the heat flared, coloring her cheeks, searing her blood.

"Don't start again, Clif."

"It started the first time I saw you, Alex."

"I have to go." She rose and hurried toward the door, but just as she reached out to close it behind her, his hand caught her wrist, holding her fast. She turned, intending to give him one of her most intimidating looks. The look turned to panic when he pulled her into his arms.

In one swift move, he twisted, pinning her against the wall.

Staring into her eyes, he ran his hands seductively along her shoulders. "I fall asleep thinking of you. An image of a red-haired witch torments me through the night. And when I wake, I wake wanting you, Alex. You," he sighed, running soft, whispery kisses across her forehead, her cheek, the corner of her mouth. "Not some imaginary lover." He circled her ear with his tongue and felt her tense beneath him. "A flesh-and-blood woman, Alex."

Running openmouthed kisses along the column of her throat, he felt her pulse fluttering. Knowing the fears she harbored, he wanted to be gentle. But the woman in his arms was so soft and warm and desirable that he felt his control slipping.

Against her throat he swore in frustration, or thought he did. "Why do you have to be so beautiful? So unattainable?"

She shivered and grasped his head, trying to bring his lips to hers, but he continued his tantalizing exploration of the delicate hollow between her neck and shoulder.

Her breathing became shallow. The blood roared in her temples, making his whispered words unintelligible.

His lips moved lower. With one hand he parted the robe. She was small, slender, perfect. With his tongue he circled her nipple, feeling it harden instantly at his touch.

He heard her gasp as his mouth covered her breast, nibbling, suckling until she writhed under him, almost sobbing his name.

Her spicy, autumn fragrance enveloped him. Her taste, her unique scent, her softness drove him to a frenzy.

Alexandra's senses whirled from the onslaught. He left her no time to think, to defend herself. Her body had become a mass of nerve endings. She felt her control snap as she gave up trying to fight both Clif and her own desire. Weakly she clung to him.

Making a slow journey across her collarbone, he brought his lips to hers at last. On a groan, his mouth savaged hers.

They clung, mouth to mouth, each needing to taste the other. Their desires drove them to a fever pitch.

Needing to feel the warmth of his flesh against hers, she slipped her hands beneath his sweater. At her touch, she heard him gasp for breath.

His hands slid beneath her parted robe, gliding across the smooth skin of her stomach. When his lips followed, he heard her little moan of protest.

She was so slender, so fragile. He felt an almost overpowering need to protect her, while at the same time wanting to devour her.

Lifting his head, he stared into her eyes—eyes that were glazed with desire.

Plunging his hands deeply into her tangled hair, he touched his lips to hers, whispering against her mouth, "Try to tell me you don't want this, Alex."

"Clif." She had to resist. She had to make him understand how important it was for her to remain in control of herself. A sob threatened to choke her. The words of protest wouldn't come. In his arms, she had lost the desire for control.

"You want me as desperately as I want you." Crushing her mouth with his, he felt himself slipping over the edge of madness.

With a final attempt at sanity, Alexandra put a hand to his mouth to stop the onslaught of drugging kisses.

"No. Please, Clif. Please stop."

He tensed. The hands at her back stilled. Taking in a deep breath, he lifted his head to stare into eyes the color of a stormy sea. Passion, desire, fear—all were evident in her gaze. He could read her wild turmoil.

"You don't mean that."

"Yes." The single word threatened to choke her. For emphasis she shook her head, sending a cloud of hair dancing on her naked shoulders.

Straightening away from her, he ran his hand roughly through his hair and swore viciously.

With shaking fingers she wiped a tear away. She wouldn't cry. She had vowed many years ago never again to cry over a man.

With one hand she clutched the lapels of the robe together. With the other she brushed a tangle of hair from her eyes. Struggling for breath, she whispered, "I'll be dressed and out of here in a few minutes."

He caught her by the shoulders and stared deeply into her eyes.

"Leave your car here. I'll drive you and Charley home."

"That isn't necessary. I can manage."

He swore. "I know you can manage, Alex. I said I'll drive you."

"But I . . ."

"We'll take care of it in the morning."

With as much dignity as she could muster, she turned away from him. On legs that felt like rubber, she walked down the hall.

Behind her, Clif stood motionless, feeling the intense energy drain from him gradually. He'd never known such need, a need bordering on insanity. He'd become obsessed with her. It was an obsession that could prove dangerous.

Chapter Nine

Clif sipped his third cup of coffee and stared bleakly out the window. He was sick of the rain. It only added to his already somber mood.

He had slept badly. Thoughts of Alexandra had flitted through his mind all night, disturbing his rest. Alexandra, fighting him in the water, yet laughing good-naturedly at his teasing. Alexandra, moving against him, responding to his kisses. Alexandra, riding beside him in silence, grudgingly allowing him to carry Charley upstairs to her bed.

MacLaren scratched at the back door, and Clif opened it to admit him. Even the puppy seemed edgy this morning.

Clif thought about the sound of Charley's laughter as they'd frolicked in the pool. It had been years since this old house had resounded with a child's laughter. It was a good sound.

He became aware of the sounds around him. The wind had whipped up, splattering rain against the windowpane. In one of the rooms upstairs, a maid ran a vacuum. On the countertop, the weatherman's voice came over the radio, predicting more rain. Except for those sounds, the house was silent and brooding.

Clif crossed to the sink and dumped the lukewarm coffee down the drain. He paused, holding the empty cup. He recalled Alexandra's voice. It was a sound like no other. Her seductive whisper. Her low, precise words of anger. Her husky laughter.

Walking from the kitchen, he held the door while MacLaren scampered through the doorway. He headed briskly for the stairs while the pup raced to keep up. The redheaded duo had bewitched him. Could he be in love? The thought caused him to clench a fist. He started up the stairs, then paused, his hand on the polished banister. In love? Impossible. He turned, stared toward the solarium, then sat down quickly on the carpeted step. The thought left him weak. In love? With whom? The sweet-tempered, animated child who made him want to give her the moon? Or the high-strung, very private woman who wouldn't let anyone get close enough to touch her, let alone to help heal old wounds?

MacLaren leaped up the stairs and scrambled onto Clif's lap, pushing his nose against the big hand that automatically began to stroke his head.

Charley was the most unspoiled, unaffected child he'd ever met. She made friends easily, putting everyone at ease in her presence. He enjoyed her company. And if he could, he'd do anything in his power to make her life easier. But that didn't constitute love, he reasoned. She was just a sweet child who brought out the best in him.

Alexandra. His hand paused in its movement until the dog nudged him. Slowly running his fingers over the sleek fur, he frowned. He couldn't afford to love her. True, she was the most beautiful woman he'd ever seen. She had a voice that made his nerves quiver, and a body that tormented him.

But she kept him at arm's length. She wouldn't confide in him. Not about her office problems, which were his business. And certainly not about her personal life, which was definitely not his business.

The investigation he had ordered at the company was continuing. He trusted the team he'd hired. But each time the evidence pointed toward Alexandra, he discounted it, hoping to find something else, someone else, to shoulder the blame. Sooner or later, a nagging little voice told him, he would have to confront her.

He was being unreasonable, he admitted. He felt an urge to protect both mother and child. And he felt good being with them. More alive, more carefree than he ever remembered feeling. But that wasn't love, he assured himself.

A frown twisted the corners of Clif's mouth. His eyes narrowed in anger. Those two little vixens. They were getting to him. He...cared very much for both of them. Trouble. The thought grew in his mind. He was beginning to care too much about those two. It could mean trouble. He would have to take extra precautions to keep them at arm's length.

It was a relief to know it wasn't love. He couldn't afford to love an employee, especially one who was the object of suspicion. Hadn't Alexandra said so herself? They couldn't afford to be involved.

Standing, he cradled the puppy in his arms and took the stairs two at a time. Passing his houseman, he gave him a muttered greeting.

"Morning, Burtan. Rotten morning, isn't it?"

As he passed, the old man turned to peer after him. Shaking his head, he continued on his way. Young Mr. Andrews seemed preoccupied these days. Of course, he'd always been deeply involved in the family business. But he seemed to take most of the problems in stride. This one must be tougher than most.

* * *

"We're cooking Thanksgiving dinner at Clif's," Charley said matter-of-factly to Milly as they scrubbed pots and pans.

Milly paused to brush a lock of damp hair from her eyes. She had dyed the carrot-colored strands to a sort of purple-hued auburn. This month her favorite color was turquoise, from her sweatshirt, pants and jogging shoes to the large hoops dangling from her earlobes.

"That's great. I figured I'd have to cook a turkey for the two of you before I drove to my sister's in Chicago." She gave the little girl a sideways glance. "Is he as good a cook as I am?"

"Well…" Charley hedged, knowing how proud Milly was of her skill in the kitchen. "He's close."

Shaking her head, Milly muttered, "Where'd she ever find one like that? Does your mother even realize what a catch that man is?"

"They're kind of funny with each other," Charley confided. She shrugged. "Like I was on the first day of school. Almost a little scared. But I think they like each other," she added quickly. "Mom tries to pretend she doesn't. But she laughs more when we're with Clif. And sometimes when he doesn't know I'm looking, I see him watching her with a funny look on his face."

"Good," Milly declared, wiping the sink and hanging the towel with a flourish. "I've always trusted my instincts. And I've liked that man from the moment I met him."

Charley headed for the door. "I've got to do my spelling. Will you hear my words?"

"Sure. Bring them down when you're ready." Milly glanced at the clock on the stove. "Did your Mom say when she'd be home?"

"She didn't know. There's a meeting after work. She figured she'd be late."

As the little girl disappeared, the old housekeeper turned off the kitchen light and walked to the empty living room. Alexandra was working much too hard lately. Milly bit her lip. It wasn't going to be easy telling Alexandra and Charley that she was thinking of moving in with her sister in Chicago. With a sigh, she snapped on the television. She'd wait until after the holidays, when she was certain of her decision. No sense burdening Alexandra with this now. Still, she thought, fiddling with the dial, if she chose to move, Charley would have to stay alone in the house from the time she got home from school until whatever time Alexandra managed to get home.

It wasn't fair, Milly thought, settling heavily into a chair. Nothing in life ever was. Her sister needed her. She couldn't refuse to help. But she loved these two people, and she knew how much they'd come to depend on her.

Milly sighed. She knew the cost of maintaining a home and educating a child. But the harder Alexandra pushed, the more debts she seemed to incur. Milly had seen the pile of bills on the dining room table. And the ancient furnace in the basement of this old gatehouse was acting up again. It was only a matter of time before it would have to be replaced with a new, modern heating unit. By the time each week's paycheck was cashed, the entire amount was spent. Alexandra would never leave this job for one that allowed her more flexibility. She'd worked too hard to get where she was. But Milly knew the amount of guilt and anxiety Alexandra suffered over missing so much of Charley's life. The older woman leaned back. She wouldn't breathe a word about Chicago until the plans were finalized. Alexandra had enough on her mind.

"Who's going to make the stuffing?" Charley asked, watching Clif wipe the inside of the turkey.

"Not me," Alexandra said, looking up from the vegetables she was chopping for a salad.

"Didn't you ever help your mother stuff a turkey?" Clif asked casually.

"Our Thanksgiving dinner used to appear magically on an elegantly set table gleaming with crystal and silver." She laughed and tore a head of lettuce. "The maids prepared the entire feast behind the closed doors of the kitchen, under the watchful eye of Norman and Sara Rose. They were in charge of the entire household staff."

Clif composed his features, hoping Alexandra hadn't seen his look of surprise. This was the first time she'd ever volunteered anything about her childhood. Keeping his tone casual, he asked, "Where did you grow up?"

"Just a mile from where I live now," she said, reaching for a crisp green pepper.

"You grew up here in Grosse Pointe?"

She nodded, then handed Charley a raw carrot stick to nibble.

"The house we live in was the gatehouse to my grandmother's estate."

"The Van Allen estate?" When she nodded her head, Clif said, "Old Charlotte Van Allen was your grandmother?"

Charley laughed. "You didn't know I'm named for my great-grandma? Charley's short for Charlotte."

The turkey was forgotten. Leaning his hip against the counter, Clif said, "That was one of the biggest estates in the area. What happened to it?"

"After she died, my—her heirs sold it to a developer."

"Did you inherit part of the estate?"

Alexandra viciously chopped at a stalk of celery. "It went to my—grandmother's daughters."

"How do you happen to own the gatehouse?"

Taking a deep breath, Alexandra said softly, "My grandmother gave it to me before she died. Most of the furniture and all of the artwork were hers. She wanted to know that her favorite things would be enjoyed, and not simply sold for their market value. She suspected that most of it would end up on the auction block.''

''I see.'' He saw a lot more than she realized. She never mentioned her mother, but simply referred to her grandmother's daughter. That told him a lot about their relationship. And Charley had been named for a generous old woman who shared Alexandra's love of art.

''When did she die?''

''Eight years ago. Two months before Charley was born.''

''So she never lived to see her great-granddaughter?'' Or to settle any money on the child, he thought grimly.

Alexandra swallowed. ''No. And Charley never had the pleasure of knowing a fascinating character.''

''You liked the old woman.'' Clif watched as she added diced cucumbers and tomato wedges to the top layer of salad.

''I adored her,'' Alexandra said.

''I've heard some pretty wild things about Charlotte Van Allen,'' Clif said as he began preparing the ingredients for the stuffing.

''Probably all of them true,'' Alexandra said with a laugh as she and Charley cleaned off the countertop.

''Did she really marry her butler after her first husband died?''

''He was her chauffeur. And that man loved her until the day he died.''

''The rumor was that he ran through her money like water through a sieve.''

''Grandmother liked to say he made some 'unwise investments.''' A frown creased Alexandra's smooth forehead. ''He was so protective of her. He knew how her family felt about him. And he knew they kept a wary eye on her estate. After he died, my mother and aunt tried to declare my grandmother incompetent, so they could take over her finances. They actually took her to court over it."

Clif nodded, trying to remember the facts as they'd been reported in the local papers. "Your grandmother won, didn't she?"

"Won?" Alexandra shrugged. "I suppose there are those who would say she won. In a family scandal like that there are no winners or losers. I've always thought the rift in the family was too painful for her to accept." Alexandra's voice lowered. "She was a flamboyant woman. She'd lived her life to the fullest. And I don't think she had too many regrets. But the loss of her daughters' love was a heartbreaker. After her death, her will was contested. The entire estate was divided between her two daughters. They liquidated everything immediately."

"Except the gatehouse."

Alexandra's eyes softened. "And a summer cottage on Torch Lake. I've been meaning to take Charley there. Someday it will be hers. Both properties had been an outright gift to me before my grandmother's death. They weren't part of her estate."

"You took your grandmother's side in the family feud, didn't you?"

Alexandra bit her lip. She'd already said more than she'd wanted to. "We were very close. There were times when I felt that my grandmother was the only one on my side."

"I'm always going to be on your side, Mom," Charley chimed in, picking up another carrot.

Feeling her heart lodge in her throat, Alexandra dropped a kiss on her daughter's head and turned toward the refrigerator, missing the wink that passed between Clif and Charley.

With a flourish, Clif laced the turkey and placed it in a roasting pan. Closing the oven, he reached for some mugs. With a glance at the rain lashing the windows, he said, "I thought about taking both of you downtown to watch the parade while the turkey cooked. But I think it would be cozier to stay indoors and watch it on TV.''

"What's that?'' Alexandra asked, as Clif poured steaming liquid into the mugs.

"Hot mulled cider.'' He added cinnamon sticks, and the spicy aroma made their mouths water. "Guaranteed to warm the cockles of our hearts. If our hearts have cockles,'' he added with a grin. "Come on, Charley,'' he said, balancing a tray. "We're going to start a blazing fire in the fireplace, and warm our toes.''

"And our hearts.''

"You already have,'' he murmured as she and her mother passed. "Just by being here.''

They settled themselves comfortably around the fireplace and watched the parade. Afterward Charley challenged Clif to a game of chess. When he realized that she was coming close to beating him, he diplomatically suggested they turn on the football game.

"But we're almost through. Two more moves, and I'll have you cornered.''

Clif grinned at the serious expression on her face. "Out for blood, aren't you?''

"My mom told me there's no point in playing unless you want to win.''

"She did, huh?'' He glanced across the room at Alexandra, who was staring silently at the flames. A drift of silky hair streamed across the cushion, catching and reflecting the fiery hue. "Didn't she ever tell you it was all right to play just for the fun of it?''

"But I am having fun. It's just more fun to beat you.''

He decided not to argue with a child's logic. "We'll pick this up later, then. Right now, I have to watch my team beat the Badgers.''

"Why didn't you go to Wisconsin with the team?" Alexandra asked as he crossed the room.

"I've had enough of holidays spent in hotels." He turned on the television. "This year, I wanted to be home."

Home. As he kicked off his shoes and stretched out between Charley and Alexandra, Clif found himself surprised by his admission. It had been years since he had wanted to spend any time here. Even in his childhood, this house had held few warm memories.

On the spur of the moment he'd decided he wanted to spend this holiday with Alexandra and Charley. He had declined his aunt's invitation to spend Thanksgiving with her. Marion would have an intimate little evening for a hundred or so of her dearest friends. As always, the talk would center on the automobile industry. Not the product, which Clif loved, but the gossip, the ugly little rumors, the snide comments about those executives who dared to break one of the rules of that conservative world. Clif knew the game. It was the same in any industry. And for the most part, he played by the rules, but he was determined to live his own life, too.

The aroma of roasted turkey filled the house. During halftime, Alexandra placed Milly's lovingly made pumpkin pie in the oven, along with sweet potatoes. Clif and Charley set the table. From the dining room Alexandra could hear their voices.

"How long have you owned the Wolverines, Clif?"

Alexandra paused at the sound of his deep voice. "Four years. Since my father died."

"Did you ever play football?"

"A little. In high school and college. But it was only a sport to me. I never took it seriously. Cars I took seriously," he added with a chuckle.

"Have the Wolverines ever made it to the Super Bowl?"

"Not yet. But if they keep up this winning streak, this could be their year."

"Who won the first Super Bowl?"

Alexandra suppressed a laugh. Leave it to Charley to ask the impossible questions.

"The Green Bay Packers."

Charley's admiration was evident in her voice. "Wow! If we play a trivia game, I hope you're on my side."

"Thanks. Maybe we can take on your mother after dinner."

"I heard that," Alexandra called. "Find yourselves another sucker."

"Next time, remember to whisper," Clif called as he walked to the fireplace and added another log.

The Wolverines won, giving Clif even more reason to celebrate. The remains of the turkey had been consigned to the refrigerator. The dishes had been stacked in the dishwasher. While Charley licked the last of the whipped cream and pumpkin pie from her lips, Alexandra placed her coffee cup on the glass-topped table and leaned back on the sofa, tucking her feet beneath her. Beside her, Clif sipped a brandy and watched as MacLaren stretched out on the other sofa next to the little girl who had won his affection.

"How'd you learn to cook, Clif?" Charley asked.

"Survival," he answered, grinning.

"What are you surviving?"

"Bachelorhood."

"What's bachelorhood?"

"The state of being unmarried."

"Then Mom's surviving bachelorhood," Charley said innocently, "but she still can't cook."

"Thank you." Alexandra stretched lazily.

Clif watched her slow movement, feeling something like a fist tighten inside him.

"You seem to have forgotten that birthday cake I made you."

"Oh, yeah. That was great," Charley said emphatically. Turning to Clif, she added, "Mom burned the cake, so she threw it out and made the entire thing out of frosting."

"And I'll bet the two of you ate the whole thing."

"Uh-hum. It was the best birthday cake I ever had."

"I'll remember not to ask you to bake me a cake."

Alexandra stood suddenly. "Since you two seem to think I'm useless, I'll carry these cups to the kitchen."

"Relax," Clif said. "Leave them for later."

"I need the exercise." Without bothering to put on her shoes, she went toward the kitchen.

"She hates to be reminded about how badly she cooks," Charley said with a laugh.

"Maybe she has too many other things to do," Clif said, watching the sway of hips that always left him feeling weak. As Alexandra disappeared into the kitchen, he said, "When she comes home from work, she has you to take care of. When I come home, I have only myself to think of."

"And MacLaren," Charley said quickly, petting the puppy.

"But MacLaren doesn't notice if the food is cooked or out of a can."

"Neither does Mom. She'd just as soon eat a peanut butter sandwich as cook something."

"That's because she pushes herself too hard." He glanced toward the closed kitchen door. "She needs someone to take care of her."

Giggling, Charley said, "Don't let my mom hear you say that."

"Say what?" Alexandra stood in the doorway.

"Nothing," Clif replied quickly.

"You need a keeper," Charley said, rolling her eyes.

At Alexandra's sharp look, Clif added, "That wasn't exactly what I said." He grinned. "But it's not such a bad idea."

"Oh, look." Charley sat up suddenly, nearly knocking MacLaren off the sofa. Pointing to the window, Charley shrieked, "Snow. The rain's turned to snow."

Running across the room, the little girl pressed her nose to the cold dark pane. "Isn't it beautiful?" She was nearly jumping up and down in her excitement. "Can we go out in it?"

Alexandra turned to Clif. Both broke into laughter at the same instant.

"Let's round up boots and gloves," Clif called, heading for the stairs. "I'll be down in a minute."

When he returned, he was dressed in a warm parka and was carrying two brightly colored scarves for mother and daughter. Throwing on switches, he flooded the grounds with light. As they stepped outside, they were struck by the beauty of the first snowfall. Already, nearly an inch of snow covered the ground, softening the landscape. The bushes and hedges wore a gauzy covering. Even the sound of an occasional car was muted by the heavy snowfall.

"Come on." Charley ran down the steps with the puppy following.

As he landed in the first drift, MacLaren yelped, then dipped his head, pushing his nose deep into the snow. Running around in circles, he explored this strange new world of frosty white.

Charley was already rolling a snowball. The damp snow was perfect for packing.

"I'm going to build a snowman. Bigger'n you, Clif."

He glanced at Alexandra. "What are we waiting for?"

During the next hour, the snowman took shape. When he was finished, he wore a bright red cap and a red-and-yellow scarf around his neck. His eyes were two dark stones, and in his mouth was a crooked stick that resembled a pipe.

"Very artistic," Clif said, stepping back to admire their handiwork.

"And very tiring. I'm about to turn into a snowman myself, if we don't get indoors soon." Despite her words, Alexandra's eyes were gleaming.

"Come on, Maclaren," Charley yelled. "One last run through the snow."

As they disappeared around the corner of the house, Clif picked up a handful of snow and caught Alexandra by the shoulder.

"Don't you dare!" Sensing his intention, she twisted loose from his grasp and started to run.

"No chance," he called, running after her. "You're not getting off this easily."

Circling a tree, she glanced over her shoulder. Seeing nothing but darkness, she laughed, thinking she'd evaded him. When she turned, she ran into a solid wall of chest.

"Clif." Her voice was breathless. "I thought you were back there."

"Wrong again." He gripped her by the shoulders and dragged her firmly against him.

"Drop the snow, Clif, or I'll . . ."

"You'll what?"

"I'll have to show you an example of my martial arts."

"I'd like that. Then I'll show you an example of my self-defense technique."

"Like this?" Alexandra lifted a hand to his throat.

"No. Like this." Dropping the snow, he cupped the back of her head and covered her lips with his.

Her laughter died in her throat. The heat of his touch shocked her. Startled, she tried to free herself, but his hands held her fast.

"Clif, I . . ."

"Shh." He brushed his lips over hers in the softest, gentlest movement. "Do you know how long it's been since I kissed a girl in the snow?"

Alexandra pretended to be shocked. "You mean there've been others?"

"None like you," he murmured, drawing her closer. "None with green eyes and apple cheeks and hair like fire."

She felt anticipation tingle through her as his lips lowered to hers. Her heart thudded against her rib cage.

His gaze centered on her lips, and she felt a hunger that was nearly physical. They came together swiftly, as if they had been waiting for this moment all evening. There was a hesitancy, a brief moment of awkwardness, as their lips touched, then parted. And then their arms were around each other, holding, clinging with a kind of mindless desperation.

Clif slipped his hands inside her jacket, drawing her even closer. The warmth of his body enveloped her as the snowflakes fell on her upturned face. With his tongue he traced the outline of her lips. She nipped his lower lip in an effort to stop his teasing movement. The tiny jolt of pain caused him to tighten his grip on her. Desire pulsed. The kiss deepened. Their tongues met, tasting the mysterious yet familiar flavors.

Clif lowered his mouth to the soft curve of her throat, and she clutched his head, tangling her fingers in his dark hair.

His hands were warm and firm as they moved up and down her sides, igniting little flames wherever they touched. She wanted him to go on kissing her, touching her, holding her. Her need for this man was frightening. No one had ever made her feel like this. He had a power over her, a power she'd vowed no man would ever wield.

He brought his lips back to hers, and she forgot all her promises. She was losing control. Losing herself to needs long suppressed. She hated herself for this weakness.

Struggling for some semblance of sanity, she brought her hands to his chest to push him away. Still holding her firmly, he raised his head.

"We have to go in now, Clif."

"Stay the night, Alex."

"That's impossible. Charley..."

"I've plenty of bedrooms."

"No. We can't. We have to get home. It's been..." She licked her lips and looked away from his intense gaze. "It's been a wonderful day, Clif."

"Stay, Alex. We'll make it a wonderful night."

She swallowed and took a step away. The sharp sting of the night air chilled her heated flesh. She felt her cool control returning. And with it, a return to reality. "I'd like to go home now," she said calmly.

She saw the anger in Clif's eyes before he caught her close and savaged her mouth with an almost brutal kiss.

"I want you, Alexandra. And you may deny it, but you want me, too."

"Haven't you learned that you can't have everything you want?"

Charley and MacLaren came crashing around the corner of the house. Before Alexandra could take a step toward them, Clif caught her roughly by the shoulder.

"One night you'll stay," he said through clenched teeth. "Because it's what we want. And I always get what I want."

She turned her back on him and caught her daughter's hand. Behind her, she could feel him watching her as she trudged through the wet snow.

Chapter Ten

We have eliminated the following employees from suspicion," the investigator said, glancing up from his report. Handing Clif a sheet of typed paper, he cleared his throat. "As you can see, Mr. Andrews, we've narrowed the field of suspects considerably."

Clif scanned the list, feeling a tightening around his heart at the exclusion of Alexandra's name. He'd hoped she would be officially cleared before this investigation went any further. They were getting dangerously close to the end of the line, and still she remained a prime suspect to some. Wordlessly he handed the sheet of paper to his aunt. Marion had insisted on being included in this briefing.

"What do you think is the motive?" Marion asked sharply.

The investigator folded his hands. "I call it the two Gs. Grudge or Greed. I've studied enough of these corporate leaks to know that money is usually the moving force. A competitor finds a key employee of yours who is living beyond his means. They make him a tempting offer. All he has to do is obtain a few secret test results, and he'll be free of debt.''

Marion's voice purred. "So if an ambitious young manager happened to want—let's say a life that's been denied her—she might be tempted to sell out the company to the highest bidder.''

Clif shot his aunt a warning look. Turning to the detective, he asked in a dangerously low voice, "Or it could be someone who bears a grudge?''

"It could be, Mr. Andrews. There's always that possibility. In either case, the name of the game is greed.'' Turning toward Marion, the detective said, "Look for an employee who enjoys the good life, or one who, through neglect or circumstances beyond his control, is deeply in debt.'' He turned to include Clif. "Or look for a disgruntled employee who feels justified in making a profit at the expense of your company.'' Spreading his palms, he said softly, "And we'll find our culprit.'' The man stood. Offering his hand, he added, "We're very close. In a matter of days or weeks, we should be able to wrap this up.'' As he walked to the door, he paused. "That thought ought to make your holidays brighter.''

When the door closed behind him, Marion returned the list of names to her nephew. "Four more employees have been eliminated. That leaves only seven or eight.'' With a look of feigned sympathy, she dropped her hand to his arm. "I noticed your Miss Porter remains a suspect.''

Though he said nothing, she noted the grim line of his mouth. She stood. "I haven't seen much of you lately, Clif.'' When he didn't respond, she added ominously, "In this town, a man's private life doesn't remain private very long.''

At his icy look, she moved toward the door. With her hand on the knob, she turned. "Will you be attending the Lake Tahoe conference with your division heads?''

"I have no choice. I'm expected to attend."

She brightened. "I haven't decided whether to attend or not. I thought I'd wait and see if anyone...interesting would be there. I'll be in touch."

When the door closed, he sat staring at a spot on the wall until the telephone shattered his gloomy thoughts.

At the frantic pounding on the door, Alexandra hurried to open it. Clif, acting very mysterious, had picked up Charley while Alexandra was still drinking her Saturday morning coffee and reading the weekend paper. They'd been gone for nearly two hours.

"Mom. Look what we bought." Charley ran in and dragged her to the door. "Look."

Clif was hauling an enormous Scotch pine up the steps.

"What in the world..."

"Your Christmas tree," he said, grinning like a school-boy. "Charley and I decided we couldn't wait any longer."

"But it's so big." She stared in dismay as he paused on the porch and righted the tree. "You'll never get it through the front door."

"Trust me." Dropping it, he grasped the trunk at the bottom and began tugging it through the narrow doorway. "Grab that other end," he ordered.

Alexandra and Charley fumbled with the branches, lifting and turning until the giant tree was through the doorway and into the living room.

While Charley ran to find newspapers and an old sheet, Clif returned with a tree stand and a small handsaw.

"Clif Andrews, that tree will never fit in this room. And you're going to destroy my carpet."

Charley and Clif knelt over the tree, pruning branches, sawing the trunk in a clean line. Looking up, Clif winked at his partner. "We'll make a believer out of her yet," he said.

"Mom. Why don't you go find the ornaments. Clif and I have a lot of work to do here."

Grumbling, Alexandra climbed to the attic and returned with a dust-covered box. The tree stood in the corner, dominating the room. A wonderful pine scent filled the house. Clif and Charley stood back, admiring their work.

"Let's hurry and get the ornaments up, Clif."

He gave Charley an indulgent smile. "These things can't be rushed. A tree this grand calls for patience. First," he said, glancing meaningfully at Alexandra, "I think the brave tree-cutters deserve a hot meal."

"Will soup and sandwiches do it?"

"I think that would save us from starvation."

"I'll call you when it's ready."

As Alexandra left the room, Charley said, "It'll be tomato soup and grilled-cheese sandwiches."

"How do you know?"

She grinned. "It's the only thing Mom knows how to make."

Twenty minutes later, Alexandra called them to the kitchen. As she ladled soup into their bowls, Clif winked at Charley. "I'll be darned. Tomato soup. What kind of sandwiches are you making?"

"Grilled cheese," Alexandra said from the stove.

"Amazing."

"What is?" She turned.

"Your daughter. She's psychic. She told me what you'd fix."

"Any grumbling in the ranks," Alexandra said, lifting an eyebrow, "and you won't get seconds." Ignoring their laughter, she put the kettle on for tea.

When they were settled around the table, Alexandra asked, "Where did you two get the tree?"

"Clif was going to take me to a farm where you cut your own." Charley gulped her milk and wiped the white mustache from her upper lip. "But it was too cold out. So we went to a place where they sell them."

"Too cold? Aren't you the two who love the snow?"

"Only if I've got someone to keep me warm," Clif murmured, reaching for a second sandwich. "These are good. What else do you make?"

"Peanut butter and jelly. And I make a great fried egg sandwich," Alexandra said in her most haughty tone.

"Didn't they teach home economics in your school?"

She smiled. "Yes. But I opted for auto mechanics."

"And Andrews Motors is grateful."

"Come on," Charley said, finishing her sandwich in one bite. "We have a lot of work to do, Clif."

"Right." He picked up his plate and placed it in the dishwasher. Pausing beside Alexandra's chair, he caught a strand of her hair and twisted it around his finger. "Coming?" he asked.

"Are you sure you want me handling those precious ornaments?"

He tugged on the lock of hair. As their eyes met, he felt his insides churn. When he was around Alexandra, desire was never far from the surface. "Of course. As long as they're not edible, we're all right."

With a shaky laugh, she turned away. "Just let me clean up in here, and I'll join you and Charley."

"Where's Milly?"

Alexandra shrugged. "She drove to Chicago again this week. Her sister hasn't been well."

"I hope it's nothing serious."

Nudging the refrigerator closed, Alexandra sighed. "She hasn't said much. But I think Milly's really worried. I should know more tomorrow. She told me she was determined to get home by Sunday."

Taking the dishes from her hands, Clif stacked them in the dishwasher and closed it. "As long as we don't have Milly around, I'll be the cook tonight."

"Who said you were invited to stay?"

He ran a finger down her nose, and saw her eyes widen in surprise. After giving her a long, lingering look, he suddenly caught her hand and led her to the living room. "I'm inviting myself."

"Oregano," Clif called. "It needs oregano."

Alexandra scoured the cupboards until she found the spices.

Clif sprinkled, stirred, tasted, then nodded. "Perfect. Here." He lifted the wooden spoon to her lips. "What do you think?"

Alexandra smiled. "I think you're amazing. Where did you ever learn to cook like this?"

"My college roommate's family owned a chain of Italian restaurants. Papa Linguini's." He grinned. "Their real name was Schultz, but that didn't matter. He had the most amazing recipes. On weekends we used to throw parties that were the talk of the campus."

"I can see you were a dedicated student."

"Dedicated to having a good time. How about you?"

"There wasn't time for parties. After class I worked. And there was Charley."

She had spoken very simply. There was no regret in her voice, yet Clif had an almost overpowering impulse to take her in his arms and kiss away the pain.

Clif glanced at the little girl who was spreading butter and garlic salt on a loaf of French bread as he had shown her. He crossed the room and tore off a sheet of aluminum foil. "Wrap it tightly, and we'll bake it for half an hour in the oven."

"That spaghetti sauce smells great, Clif. When will it be ready?"

"Soon. Now for the best part. We get to make the dessert." He tore open a bag of caramels and dumped them into a pan. "We'll have to stir constantly so they don't burn on the bottom."

"I'll stir," Alexandra offered. "You two get to peel the apples."

When the apples were peeled and sliced, Clif dropped them into the melted caramel mixture. Laying them out on a sheet of waxed paper, he set them on the windowsill. "It's cooler here," he explained. "They won't be so sticky."

"This is too fine a meal to be eaten in the kitchen," Alexandra declared. "We'll make it a party. I'm setting the dining room table."

A short time later they sat down to a wonderful meal of pasta with spicy tomato sauce and salad, accompanied by warm garlic bread.

"I hope Milly doesn't ask me what we ate while she was gone," Charley said earnestly. "She'll be jealous when I tell her Clif's the best cook in the world."

"I think you'd better keep that comment to yourself," Alexandra mused.

"But I thank you for the compliment," he said, chuckling. "How about having our dessert and coffee in the living room, where we can admire our tree."

Alexandra blinked, wondering if she was the only one who noticed Clif's use of the term "our" tree.

In the front room, they plugged in the multicolored lights and curled up on the sofa to enjoy the effect.

"It needs something," Clif commented, reaching for a caramel-coated apple slice.

"The angel." Alexandra stood and hurried from the room. A minute later she returned, carrying a tissue-wrapped figure. Unwrapping it, she handed it to Charley. "I think you should place the angel on top."

"I can't reach."

Clif picked her up and lifted her high in the air. "Wow! I can reach clear to the top of the tree!" she cried, setting the porcelain angel on the highest branch.

Seeing her daughter in Clif's arms, Alexandra felt a twinge of regret. They were so warm, so natural with each other. A father image was the one thing that had been missing in her daughter's life. What would happen to Charley when Clif walked away?

Angrily she dismissed the fear. He was good company. Nothing more.

The three of them stood back, admiring.

"It still needs something," Clif muttered.

"Popcorn."

Clif and Charley looked at Alexandra.

"I'll get out the corn popper. We'll string popcorn. It makes a wonderful decoration for the tree."

Soon the scent of hot butter and popcorn filled the house. With needles and thread, the three of them sat on the floor around a huge bowl.

While Charley diligently threaded the fluffy kernels on a string, Clif sat beside her, sliding them off the other end and popping them into his mouth. When she finally caught him, she squealed, "Clif. I can't believe you. Mom, he's eating my popcorn faster'n I can string it."

"That's for eating," Alexandra said, indicating the bowl. "This is for stringing." She pointed to the popcorn that dangled from Charley's needle. "If you two keep up this teasing, we'll never finish decorating the tree."

But the good-natured banter continued, with Charley giggling each time she caught Clif eating the popcorn off her string. Watching them, Alexandra wondered if she'd ever seen her daughter happier. Clif had a way of bringing out the very best in her.

Seeing the look on Alexandra's face, Clif held out a piece of popcorn. She accepted it. His fingers lingered a second against her lips, sending tiny shivers along her spine. When she glanced at him, he could read the surprise in her eyes.

"One more strand should do it," Clif called a few minutes later as he draped the string of popcorn around the tree branches.

"I'm afraid it's going to have to wait for another day," Alexandra said softly.

As Clif turned, she pointed to her daughter, whose head bobbed slightly over the popcorn bowl. Charley's eyelids were already too heavy to hold open.

"Come on," Clif said, lifting her gently in his arms. "We have to save something for another day. Time for bed."

Wrapping her arms around his neck, she gave a last glance at the glittering tree. "It's the best tree we've ever had, Clif."

"Wait till you see the one we get next year," he murmured against her cheek. "It'll be even better."

Struck by his words, Alexandra went rigid. She felt as if she had just been slammed into a brick wall. Next year. He had spoken those words as casually as if their future was already settled. Next year and all the years to come. What a lovely dream. And he was cruelly holding out that fantasy to an innocent child, only to snatch it from her grasp.

Alexandra berated herself. She'd let down her guard and allowed him to get too close. Despite all her precautions, she'd fallen in love with Clif Andrews. She'd allowed herself and her daughter to begin believing in...in Santa Claus. Fool. Hadn't she already had a taste of that kind of foolishness? Love. Her hand gripped the banister until the knuckles were white. It was time to deal honestly with her feelings. She felt her knees tremble slightly. She swallowed. It was time to be honest with Clif and send him on his way.

Time to forget any silly romantic notions. Then she could get back on track, sticking to the goals she'd set for herself.

She paused in midstride, staring silently at his broad shoulders as he climbed the stairs. Then, biting her lip, she followed.

Clif deposited Charley in her bed and touched his lips to her cheek.

"Want to help me make breakfast in the morning?" she asked.

"I wouldn't miss it."

"Night, Clif," she mumbled as he walked from the room. Her mother helped her slip out of her clothes. Minutes later, she was sound asleep.

Downstairs, Clif poured two glasses of pale wine and turned off the lamps, so that the only illumination came from the tiny jeweled lights of the tree.

At the sound of Alexandra's footsteps, he turned with a smile. Seeing her stiff features, he watched her, puzzled.

"We have to talk, Clif."

When he offered her a glass of wine, she refused. "What I have to say requires a clear head. And please," she said quickly as he opened his mouth, "no interruptions."

She paced the room in agitation, while Clif watched in silence. Crossing her arms over her chest, she turned to face him.

"Charley has begun to look forward to your visits."

A smile tugged at the corner of his lips. "And you haven't."

She tossed her head. "Yes. I...I admit I enjoy having you here, too. But it's Charley I'm worried about. She's so young, so vulnerable. I won't have her hurt."

"How am I going to hurt her?" His tone was angrier than he'd intended.

"She's going to learn to count on you. And then one day you're going to walk out of her life, as easily as you walked in."

He went very still. "Is that what happened, Alex?" His voice was so low she had to strain to hear it.

"We're talking about you, Clif. Not me."

"We seem to be talking about your expectations. Do you feel you have to get hurt in a relationship, Alex? Can there be no happy endings?"

"Happy endings." For a moment he saw her lower lip tremble. He thought her eyes filled with tears, but she swung away too quickly for him to be sure.

With her back to him, she said, "I gave up believing in happy endings a long time ago. I've been able to cope with reality for a long time now. I want Charley to be able to deal with it, too."

"Just what is reality, Alexandra?" His tone was softer now as the anger drained away, leaving fear in its place.

She didn't seem to notice. Turning, she gave him a cool look. "Reality is having your own parents turn against you when you make a mistake. Reality is having to get up at dawn to study for exams because your baby is teething and couldn't settle down to sleep. Reality is taking a second part-time job because one job just won't pay the bills."

His hands clenched at his sides. He forced his tone to remain even. "Do your parents know how tough it's been?"

She clutched her arms about herself, suddenly cold. "No. And I'll never tell them."

"Too proud?"

"Call it what you want. I can take care of myself."

"What about Charley's father? Has he offered to help?"

He saw her stiffen. Very deliberately, she dropped her hands to her sides. He saw them ball into fists.

"Charley has no father."

"Alex, it takes two..."

"I know what it takes," she spat. "I found out the hard way." Lowering her head, she stared at a spot on the carpet. In a monotone, she said, "It's a story as old as time. I was young and innocent. And he was knowledgeable—and very persuasive. The minute I gave in, he lost interest. And when I found myself carrying his child, he suggested that there were probably plenty of men around to share the guilt. He knew better, of course. But I realized just how low he was. And I knew I wanted no further contact with him. I never saw him again. I never want to."

Clif stood quietly, hating the nameless, faceless man who had inflicted such pain. "Your family..."

"My family was no better." Alexandra wondered at the pain she still felt at the very mention of her parents. "My mother called me unspeakable names and suggested that I'd caused my father's heart attack. They were horrified when I announced that I intended to keep my baby. They accused me of wanting to humiliate them publicly. Within six months they had sold everything here and moved to the Coast."

"Where did you go?"

"Gram took me in, even though she'd just lost her husband." Alexandra felt tears coming and blinked them back. She wouldn't cry. "My mother never forgave her for it. She accused my grandmother of corrupting my morals."

"That's why she was dragged through the courts?"

She wiped her damp lashes, hating her weakness. "I've always thought that was the real reason. They disapproved of Gram's life-style. They decided mine was no better. My family wanted to punish her for taking my part."

Alexandra wrapped her arms about herself and was surprised at how cold her hands were. Clif fought the desire to hold her. Walking closer, he handed her a glass of wine.

"Here. You're shivering."

She seemed surprised at his concern. Taking a sip of the pale liquid, she glanced up. "Now that you've heard my story, you can leave."

"Why would I leave?"

"Because you know the truth."

"And you think the truth will drive me away?"

"Of course." It had driven away everyone else who knew.

As she watched in surprise, he took the glass from her hands. Placing it on a table, he turned back and took her in his arms. With his lips pressed to her forehead, he murmured, "Thank you for telling me. You didn't have to."

She tried to fight the weakness she felt at his simple touch. "Yes, I did. You deserved that much."

"But I want more, Alexandra. Much more."

As she opened her mouth to protest, he covered her lips in a searing kiss.

Caught by surprise, she pressed her hands against his chest, trying to push him away. But at the first touch of his lips to hers, she lost the will to resist.

"Clif."

"Don't say any more," he whispered against her mouth. "Just let me love you."

Despite the urgency of the kiss, she hesitated. But his lips were warm, persuasive. The hands at her back were strong and firm. He moved his mouth to her cheek, to the sweep of her eyebrow, to the little pulse at her temple. Soft, feathery kisses soothed away her fears until she felt herself trembling from his tenderness.

Slowly her hands curled into the front of his shirt. She felt the hard angles and planes of his body melting into the softness of hers. Her arms reached up to circle his neck. His lips covered hers, warm and sweet.

His hand slid under her sweater, trailing the satin softness of her back. He cupped her breast and heard her sudden intake of breath. She was small and firm and perfectly formed. As he took the kiss deeper, he lost all ability to think. He knew only that he wanted her, as he'd never wanted anyone.

When his mouth left hers to trail along her neck and nuzzle the sensitive little hollow of her shoulder, she felt her blood turn to a river of fire. His lips, his fingertips, caused ripples of pleasure inside her, left her knees weak. He murmured her name and brought his lips to hers.

Her soft scent surrounded him, seducing him. "I want you, Alexandra." The words were torn from his throat. "I can't take any more of this. I want you. All of you. Your heart, your mind, your body."

Alexandra's heartbeat thundered in her ears. They were treading on dangerous ground. Each time they came together, she lost a little more of herself.

"No." She took a step backward. Her legs were like rubber, and the floor seemed to tilt and sway. "Never." She felt the blood rush to her head and lifted her hands to her cheeks.

"Don't deny what we both feel." He caught her by the arm, but she spun away, out of his reach.

"I want you to leave, Clif."

His voice lowered dangerously. "The hell you do. We can have the night, Alex."

"And in the morning?"

"Charley and I will make breakfast. We'll finish the tree. We'll..."

"We'll play house, is that it?" She lowered her voice to barely a whisper. "You have no place in our lives, Clif. No one does. I want you to leave. Now."

"I'm good for you, Alex. For you and Charley."

"Leave her out of it. Don't play games with me, Clif. Just leave."

He took a step closer, catching her roughly by the shoulders. His voice was a low rasp of fury. "I don't want to leave, Alex. I want to stay. Tonight and every night. I want to be with you and Charley.''

For a long moment she seemed unable to fight his hypnotic pull. Then slowly, as if in a daze, she pushed herself away from him.

Her green eyes were dark with anger. ''I believed that lie once, Clif. Afterward, I vowed I'd never let anyone hurt me like that again. I want you to leave.''

He reached out a hand to her hair, and she turned on him like a wild creature.

''No more sweet words. No more empty promises. Just go, Clif. I've allowed this to go too far. From now on, our relationship is strictly business.''

He dropped his hand to his side. His eyes were narrowed with anger. ''Do you really think the two of us can just turn away from what's already between us?''

''There is nothing between us. And there never will be.''

His features were grim. But something in his eyes spoke of determination. ''We'll see about that.''

Long after he'd stalked from the house, she continued to stand in the center of the living room. The only sound was her unsteady breathing as she fought back her tears.

Chapter Eleven

I hate to ask this, Milly, but I'm expected to attend a conference next week. Will you be here?''

The older woman stirred the soup before turning with a careful smile. This wasn't the time to burden Alexandra with her problems. ''The timing is perfect. My sister is waiting for the results of her latest tests. She plans to spend the week resting from her trip to the hospital. So Charley can spend the whole week at my place.''

''That's wonderful. I really appreciate this, Milly.''

''Where will you be going?''

''Lake Tahoe.''

''How romantic.'' The older woman gave a long sigh. ''Ski trails, sleigh bells, roaring fires.''

''Try workshops, panel discussions and dry speeches. I'll probably never even find time to leave the hotel.''

''Make the time. You may never get a chance like this again.''

"Oh, Milly, I wish you could go in my place. I'd much rather be home."

As she picked up her briefcase, Alexandra wondered how she would handle being in the same hotel with Clif for days on end. Since that last night at her house, they had been cordial but distant at the office. And she had made certain that she was never alone with him. Fortunately, they wouldn't be flying out together. She'd heard that Clif was leaving early on the company jet, and she was taking a commercial flight a day later.

When she reached the office, Alexandra found Bill Campbell standing just inside her door.

"Looking for me, Bill?"

He glanced up quickly. Jamming his hands into his pockets, he scowled. "Your assistant. Where is he?"

She shrugged. "Mike's usually early. Maybe he's getting some coffee. I'll tell him you're looking for him."

He seemed to hesitate a moment, then sauntered away.

Sitting down, Alexandra sorted through her mail and frowned when she found a memo requesting her presence in the president's office at noon. Setting it aside, she tore open an envelope marked "Top Secret Test Results" and scanned the report. When she was done, she took a small key from her briefcase and unlocked a drawer. Filing the secret document, she locked the drawer and attacked the rest of the mail.

"Good afternoon, Miss Porter. Mr. Andrews is expecting you. Please go right in."

"Thank you, Martha."

"Oh, Martha." Marion stepped off the executive elevator and brushed past Alexandra. "I must see my nephew right away."

"I'm sorry. He has an appointment right now. If you'd care to wait . . ."

"I'll only be a minute. I'm sure you don't mind." Giving Alexandra a measured look, Marion motioned for a beautiful blond woman to follow her.

"Mr. Andrews, your aunt would like a minute of your time," Martha said, reaching the doorway a moment before the others.

"What is it, Marion?"

As she waited just beyond the doorway, Alexandra was aware of the note of impatience in his tone.

"Clif, you remember Marguerite Van Horn. She was your guest at a football game a while back."

Her words brought an unexpected stab to Alexandra's midsection. Jealousy? It was a feeling she'd never known, one she sought instantly to reject.

Glancing over her shoulder, Marion shot Alexandra a triumphant look. "Marguerite and I thought it would be fun to get in some skiing. So we've decided to go with you to the sales conference next week. I'm sure you won't mind if she comes along on the company plane."

Clif barely glanced up. "That's fine, Marion. Miss Van Horn is welcome. Now if you'll excuse me."

Marion's voice lowered. "I thought you'd join us for lunch."

Clif sat back and met his aunt's frown of annoyance. Beside her, Marguerite pouted. "Maybe another time. I'm afraid I'm too busy today."

For some strange reason Alexandra felt a rush of relief at his curt dismissal of them.

"I'm beginning to think a trip to Tahoe will do you good, Clif," Marion huffed. "We'll get you out on the slopes and teach you how to have fun."

Turning, Marion gave Alexandra a last lingering look before leading her guest back to the elevators.

As she took a tentative step into the office, Alexandra heard the door close softly behind her. Glancing up, she saw

Clif watching her from the high-backed chair behind his desk.

"You wanted to see me, Mr. Andrews?"

How long was she going to continue this game? he wondered with a flash of annoyance. "Yes, Miss Porter. Have a seat."

She sat stiffly, gripping the arms of the chair as if poised to run.

"As you know, the final test results are in from Emmet's department."

"Yes. My copy arrived this morning."

"Since all of our division heads will be out of town next week, we won't have time to discuss the outcome of these tests until we return. I'd prefer that they not be discussed with personnel from the other divisions at the conference."

She nodded as she continued to look at him.

Damn her for being so beautiful, he thought, clenching a fist. Or worse, for being so cool. "I'd like you to arrange a meeting for top-level management as soon as possible after the sales conference."

She lifted an eyebrow, considering. "All right. If you think I should. Will there be anything else?"

She saw the hardness come into his eyes. "Nothing else."

If only she could forget how he looked when he smiled at her. If only she could forget the way his lips felt on hers, the touch of his hands on her skin. Taking in a deep breath, she promised herself that if it took a lifetime, she would erase all thought of him.

As she stood and walked to the door, he said softly, "What arrangements have you made for Charley while you're away?"

She forced herself to turn and meet his look. "She isn't your concern."

"I know that, damn it," he snapped. Then, taking a deep breath, he said calmly, "I just wondered if Milly was still in Chicago."

Alexandra softened her tone slightly. "Milly's back. She'll keep Charley at her place for the week."

He nodded. "I'm glad."

Don't be, she thought. *Don't care about us. Don't think about us. And in time, we'll all go back to the way we were. Before I realized I love you.*

Without another word, Alexandra pulled open the door and closed it firmly behind her.

Her briefcase had been rifled. One look, and Alexandra knew that someone had rearranged the papers inside. The document that had been on the top of the pile of papers was now at the very bottom. She reached farther, and her fingers froze. The key was missing. Alexandra took everything out of her briefcase, scattering the contents across the top of her desk. The key to her file drawer, which she always kept in a pocket of her briefcase, wasn't there.

"Spring cleaning?" Mike asked, walking into her office.

"Someone stole my key." She looked up, exasperated.

"What's it for?"

"A drawer."

Seeing a glint near his feet, Mike bent and picked up a small silver key. "This it?"

"Oh." She accepted it and gave a long sigh of relief. "My lifesaver. Thanks." Had she been mistaken? Had she, in her haste, dropped the key this morning? As her heartbeat returned to normal, she stared at the jumble of papers on her desk and muttered, "I wish I hadn't been so quick to dump all this." Now she wasn't so sure if her papers had been rearranged.

"I'll help you."

As Mike began handing the papers to her, she asked, "Did you see anyone in my office while I was out?"

"No." He paused. "Wait. I did see Bill Campbell walking out a while ago."

"He was looking for you," she said absently, stacking the papers into some semblance of order. "I forgot to tell you. He was in here early this morning hoping to find you."

"Odd," Mike said. "He didn't mention it."

As her assistant walked back to his desk, Alexandra paused in her work. There were too many coincidences. As soon as she returned, she would have to report her suspicions to the board.

"You've got to take this sweater," Charley insisted. "It's my favorite."

"All I need are a couple of silk blouses and two suits. I'm not going on vacation, honey. This is a working conference."

"Mom." Reversing their roles, Charley folded the sweater and added a pair of elegantly tailored slacks, as well as her mother's favorite jeans. "If you get a few minutes to yourself, you're going to want to walk through the town, or go skiing, or shopping." She grinned. "And if you happen to see a pair of skis just my size . . ."

"Think they'd fit in a suitcase?" Alexandra ruffled her daughter's hair and gave her a hug. "What are you and Milly planning for the week?"

"She's got tickets to a local ballet, and she promised to take me shopping. And we're definitely baking brownies."

"Umm. Save one for me. Sounds like you're going to be busy."

"Maybe you'd better stay away for two weeks."

"Sounds like you're anxious to get rid of me."

In reply, her daughter gave her a kiss on the cheek.

At the last minute, Alexandra threw in a couple of silk dresses. There would, after all, be dinners at the hotel. She closed her luggage and hauled it down the stairs. At the doorway she hugged her daughter fiercely.

"Oh, I'm going to miss you so much."

"Me, too, Mom. But don't worry about me. Milly and I will be fine."

"I know you will. I'll see you Friday night."

As the cab pulled away from the curb, Alexandra turned and waved until the pint-sized image of herself was out of sight.

Alexandra had never seen anything quite so glorious. The hotel was a granite-and-glass contemporary design nestled in the basin of a crystal lake. Behind it towered the Sierra Nevada. At dawn she stood at the window, watching streaks of mauve and pink slash the horizon. The sky gradually changed from gray to pearl, and then to clear bright blue. When the sun rose higher, it glistened on a world of dazzling white. As the town slowly awoke, skiers could be seen flashing along the powdery slopes.

Enjoying a leisurely cup of coffee in her room, Alexandra cast envious glances at the vacationers who could indulge in such luxury. Within an hour, her workday would begin; it would end only after a late-night buffet featuring dry business speeches.

The week had passed quickly. Although she often saw Clif seated with other executives, she'd had no opportunity to speak to him. But several times during workshops, she'd felt his gray eyes carefully appraising her as she sat with the other managers.

Often she found herself wondering if he went skiing with his aunt and the beautiful blonde who'd accompanied them. Twice she had seen them at dinner with a host of other executives. The elegant woman beside him looked as if she'd always belonged in his world of success and luxury.

Though she felt her heart splintering into little pieces, she reminded herself that this pain was nothing compared with what she would have suffered if she had let their relationship continue. She and Charley would never fit into Clif's world. Her past would always be a shadow on an ambitious executive's bright future.

Today would be her last day here. She looked longingly at the faded denims hanging in the closet. There had been no chance to unwind, to walk along a snow-covered lane, to curl up by the fireplace in the skiers' lounge.

She showered and dressed quickly, checking the schedule of the day's events. There was a round-table discussion over brunch, and two workshops she was required to attend before dinner. If she pushed, she might find time to slip out of the hotel and shop for something for Milly and Charley.

As she walked toward the bank of elevators, she heard the bell signaling their arrival. Breaking into a run, she slipped inside just as the elevator doors were closing. Slightly breathless, she found herself face-to-face with Clif Andrews.

"Good morning."

She mentally cursed the flush that stole across her throat and colored her cheeks. He looked wonderful. His hair still glistened from a recent shower. He smelled faintly of lemon and tangy after-shave. "Good morning."

"Have you been having a good time?"

She'd smile if it killed her. "Wonderful. And you?"

"Great. Very relaxing."

"We've had fresh snow every day. I'm sure the slopes are fast."

"Probably."

She glanced up suddenly. "Haven't you been on them?"

He gave her what he hoped was a bland look. "I came here to work."

"I thought..." She felt her color deepening and stared at the numbers flashing above the door.

When he touched her arm, she pulled back.

"What time is your flight, Alex?"

She swallowed. "Nine o'clock."

His voice lowered seductively. "Have a drink with me before you leave."

"There isn't time." And she couldn't allow herself to be alone with him. She couldn't. Her feelings were too strong. She had a fleeting image of herself at eighteen, so trusting, so naive.

"Make time," he said through clenched teeth.

Alexandra's thoughts flew to Milly. Make time. Hadn't Milly given her that same advice?

Noting her awkward pause, Clif pressed on. "Six o'clock. Suite twelve-fourteen."

The doors opened, and several people stepped into the elevator. Alexandra felt the heat of Clif's body as he moved closer, brushing against her. Glancing up, she found him staring down at her. Fixing her gaze straight ahead, she tried to ignore him, but she knew his penetrating eyes were still watching her.

When they stopped at the main floor, he leaned forward to whisper "I'll be expecting you."

She charged ahead, joining the crowd that was filing into a ballroom. When at last she took her seat at a table, Clif was nowhere to be seen.

The closed suitcases rested beside the bed.

Alexandra studied her reflection in the mirror, wondering if Clif would see the fear in her eyes. She was a fool to go to his suite, she told herself again. But she wasn't strong enough to stay away. She wanted to see him.

The woman in the mirror was sophisticated without being sleek. Her dress was of emerald silk, with a softly draped bodice and a low back that dipped nearly to the waist, making it impossible to wear anything beneath it. Over this, she wore a matching silk jacket. The pearls at her throat and earlobes had been her grandmother's. She had swept her hair into a coil at the back of her head and fastened it with a mother-of-pearl comb. With a last glance at her makeup, she picked up a small beaded bag and walked to the door.

Shirtless, Clif stood by the window, watching the skiers make their way down the lighted slopes. Why was there never time enough to do the things he wanted? He took a long drag on his cigarette, then stubbed it in the ashtray. It would be wonderful to spend the weekend here, skiing, relaxing, talking and laughing with Alexandra, away from the pressures of home and business. But that wall she'd built around herself made it impossible.

Crossing to the closet he took a clean shirt off the hanger and slid it over his still-damp skin. As he began to button it, he paused. He couldn't fault her for the way she behaved. She'd been burned. What she was doing was a matter of self-preservation. After tucking the shirt into the waistband of his trousers, he began carefully knotting his tie. It was obvious, more than obvious, that Alexandra wasn't frigid. But she was a woman who needed commitment from a man. His hand paused in midair. Marriage. The beginnings of a smile curled the corners of his mouth. If they were married, their lives would be complete. She could respond like the woman she was, without guilt. With her and Charley, he would have the family he'd always dreamed of. Clif grinned at his reflection in the mirror. Could he pull it off? He gazed out the window for long minutes. He was a man accustomed to having what he wanted. And he wanted Alexandra as he'd never wanted anyone, anything in his life. There was a chance, just a chance, that he could have it all.

Pulling on his suit jacket, Clif smoothed his hair and hurried to answer the door. A waiter entered, with a tray of hors d'oeuvres and a bottle of chilled champagne. When the waiter left, Clif lit another cigarette. He was as nervous as a cat. A plan was forming in his mind. He was going to have to be very careful and very persuasive.

"Right on time," he said, opening the door on her first knock.

"I can't stay long," she said as she entered. "The closing dinner is in an hour."

"I'll take your jacket. It's warm in here."

Alexandra began to remove her jacket, then thought better of it. There was no sense living dangerously. "I'll keep it on. I'm feeling chilly."

Clif shrugged and crossed the room to pour two glasses of champagne. "Maybe this will warm you."

She accepted and felt a tiny thrill as their fingers touched. Glancing up, she felt a momentary jolt at the look in his slate eyes. There was something there, something unreadable.

She walked to the window to put some distance between them. "Have you and Monique been enjoying yourselves here?"

"You mean Marguerite?"

She shrugged and avoided looking at him. "Whatever."

Clif smiled at her rigid back. She wasn't going to make it easy for him. "Tahoe is a very romantic place. It would be impossible for the right man and woman not to have a good time."

His words hurt more than she would have believed possible.

"Would you like to try the caviar? Maybe the Brie?" He held out the tray of hors d'oeuvres.

"No, thank you." She'd choke on them, she thought. She shouldn't have come. This was too painful.

"Have you had a chance to try the slopes?"

She shook her head. "No time."

"How about the gaming tables?"

She smiled. "I decided to gamble twenty dollars at a blackjack table. It took me about five minutes to lose it. I decided I work too hard for my money to be a gambler."

He chuckled, a warm, vibrant sound that touched a nerve deep inside her. "What you need is a good-luck charm."

"Do you have one?"

"I am one. Everything I touch at the tables turns to gold."

"I'll remember that the next time I'm coming to Tahoe."

"Why not take advantage of my offer this trip?"

She shrugged and took a step away. He was too close, too virile. "There's no time left to gamble. This trip's over in a matter of hours."

"We could change that."

She went very still. For a moment she couldn't believe what he'd said. Turning she met his opaque gaze. "My flight leaves tonight."

"Tickets can be changed. I could have the company jet return for us on Sunday night."

"Us? What are you saying?" A little of the champagne sloshed over the rim of her glass. She didn't even notice.

"I'm asking you to stay the weekend with me."

"Clif, we've been over all this. When are you going to..."

"We're in Nevada, Alexandra. There's a little wedding chapel just down the street."

"Wedding..." More champagne spilled.

Clif took the glass from her hand and set it on a mirrored table. "This was made for drinking, not watering the carpets." Catching her hands in his, he felt the trembling she couldn't control. "I love you, Alex. And it must be obvious that I adore Charley."

"I'm very grateful that you feel that way about her, Clif, but ..."

"I don't want your gratitude." His voice was rough with emotion. Drawing her closer, he breathed, "I want you. Since I first laid eyes on you, Alex, I've wanted you desperately."

"But that isn't a reason to marry."

"Isn't it?" He gripped her shoulders almost painfully and stared down into her wide eyes. "Haven't you noticed? I'm obsessed with you. I can't sleep, I can't eat and I can't work because of you. You've taken over my life, Alexandra." His lips closed over hers with a possessiveness she'd never felt before. At once her blood heated, her lips answered. Bringing her hands to his shoulders, she fought back her fears.

Wasn't this what she'd always dreamed of? Wasn't this what she had always known would be hers if she waited? Why then was she feeling so disoriented?

"Clif." She drew a little away, needing time, needing space. "We need to think about this. Marriage is a big step."

"I don't need time. I need you." He touched her cheek, running his knuckles over the smooth skin. "I'm a selfish man, Alex. I've always gotten what I wanted. And I want you," he growled against her mouth, drawing her firmly against him.

His hands pressed her hips to his, then roamed her sides, pausing at the swell of her breasts. She gave a little sigh, and he took the kiss deeper. His thumbs stroked her until she thought she'd go mad.

Alexandra felt herself being swept along on a tide of emotions that left no room for debate. He loved her. She loved him. The man she loved as much as life itself wanted to marry her.

"Say the word, and we'll be married now," he murmured against her lips.

"You mean right now?"

"This minute." Still holding her firmly, he lifted his head. His eyes met hers.

"Oh, Clif." She clutched his arm, feeling a wave of panic.

He glanced down at her tenderly. "Unless, of course, you're having second thoughts."

Second thoughts? She'd had a million thoughts—and arguments with herself—about the wisdom of loving Clif. The fact was beyond her control. She already loved him desperately. What she had adamantly refused to allow herself to dream about was marriage to him. It had been too unattainable. Could they be good for each other? Could it work? She had to take the chance.

She swallowed and touched a hand to his cheek. When at last her words came out, they were surprisingly clear. "I'm certain if you are."

He brought her palm to his lips and lovingly kissed each finger while continuing to gaze into her eyes. "I've never been more sure of anything in my life."

The hotel limousine swept along the snow-covered highway. In the beam of headlights, snowflakes swirled and danced.

How could this be? Alexandra thought, dazed. A half hour ago she'd been Miss Alexandra Porter. Now, after a brief ceremony in front of a justice of the peace, she was Mrs. Clifton Quin Andrews.

"I'm sorry about the ring."

She forced herself out of her reverie and glanced at the oversize college ring on her left hand. "A little bigger, and I could wear it as a bracelet."

"There's a vault filled with jewelry in Michigan." He lifted her hand to his lips, and she felt a sudden rush of heat. Would he always have this effect on her? Would he always be able to set her on fire with a mere touch? "But I want to buy you something new—something of your own." Something that didn't have any associations with his parents, Clif thought.

Her voice was husky. "I suppose your aunt would object to my having anything of her family's."

"Marion has nothing to say about our lives," he said sharply.

Alexandra lapsed into silence. Marion would be shocked by the news of their marriage, of course. And, Alexandra was certain, Marion would never accept it. How deeply would that affect Clif?

When the limousine passed the hotel entrance, Alexandra was surprised. "Where are we going?"

"To a private chalet. I've had our luggage taken there already."

"So that no one from the company will see us?"

"That isn't the reason. They've all gone home by now. But I don't want to share you with anyone."

Alexandra shivered as the driver opened the door. Stepping out, Clif lifted her in his arms and carried her through the doorway of a luxurious chalet, where a fire crackled invitingly. Instead of setting her down, he continued to the bedroom, where he finally put her on her feet beside a massive king-size bed.

Seeing the bed, she felt suddenly as shy and awkward as a teen.

"I'd better phone Charley and tell her I won't be home until Sunday."

"We can both tell her the good news."

Alexandra's eyes widened. Her hand flew to her mouth. "Tell Charley." For a moment she looked absolutely terrified. "Clif, I don't think this is something we can tell her on the phone."

He touched a fingertip to her lips. "All right. Whatever you think, Alex. While you're phoning Charley, I'll pour the champagne."

On a linen-covered table drawn up before the fire, a sumptuous wedding supper had been arranged. In the center, masses of orchids formed an exotic bouquet. From an ice bucket, Clif lifted a bottle of champagne and filled two glasses.

"I'll see you Sunday night, then. I love you."

Replacing the receiver, Alexandra turned and accepted one of the crystal glasses. With a finger, Clif traced the tiny frown line between her brows.

"Trouble?"

A smile replaced the frown. "I guess I'm feeling a little slighted. I forgot about the time difference. Charley didn't even ask why I'm staying on. She was too eager to leave for the ballet."

"Then you can relax, knowing your daughter is having a good time without you."

She nodded, then looked up to meet his cool silver gaze. Again she felt the heat. He needed only to look at her, and she felt her bones melting.

"It's so warm in here. Must be the fire."

As she touched her cheek, his gaze slid to her jacket. Taking the glass from her hand, he set it on the table and slipped the silk covering from her shoulders. Draping it on a chair, he turned and realized that her dress was backless.

Running his hand lightly along her back, he murmured, "It's a good thing I didn't know about this earlier. We never would have made it to the chapel."

"Sorry I kept it from you?"

His hands went to her hair, drawing out the comb that held it up. Her hair tumbled about in shimmering waves that kissed her cheeks and danced lightly on her shoulders.

"You've kept so much from me, Alex," he murmured, plunging his hands into the rich, auburn cloud. "So much." He covered her lips with his, and the flame grew. Bringing his hands to her waist, he found the zipper. A drift of emerald silk whispered to the floor. For long moments he gazed at her body. "You're so perfect." His tongue traced the outline of her lips, and he felt her tremble. "Don't ever keep anything from me again." His husky voice thrilled her as he brought his lips to the hollow of her throat.

His hands moved over her body, leaving her trembling with desire. Passion built until it was almost pain.

"Oh, Clif. I love you so much." Her words were breathless. "Love me. Love me."

She didn't remember being carried to the bed. She knew only that she was surrounded by silk sheets and satin quilts. She couldn't recall how she shed his clothes. She knew only that he lay beside her, flesh to flesh, heartbeat to heartbeat. There was no patience, no gentleness. They came together in a frenzy.

His hands moved over her, exploring, possessive. His lips followed, needing to taste her, to know every part of her intimately. A longing sprang from deep inside her, turning her bones to liquid, her blood to molten lava. His hands caressed the smooth, satin flesh of her stomach, then moved up to cup the swell of her breasts. A moment later they were replaced by his lips, teasing her already hard nipples. Hearing her moan of pleasure, he kissed her throat, where he felt her pulse throb.

All her shyness disappeared. Her hands explored his body, thrilling to the muscles of his shoulders and back. Moving her hands along his sides, she felt his narrow hips, the flat plane of his stomach. As she brought her hand lower, he gave a desperate moan and savaged her mouth.

She thrilled to the power she had over him. Bolder now, she let her fingertips begin a slow mesmerizing journey of discovery.

His touch became wild, demanding. Her scent, that exotic autumn scent that was uniquely hers, surrounded him, filled all his senses, until her essence was part of him, crowding out all thought.

His mouth found hers, and he prolonged the kiss until all she could taste was him, dark, musky, completely masculine.

Their bodies joined, and they tumbled into a world of sensation. He called her name and whispered words that she could no longer hear. But she knew their meaning. Clinging tightly, she moved with him, her hands clasped about his neck. A fine sheen covered their bodies. Inexorably, passion built until they felt themselves exploding in a shower of stars.

He was hers. Even while she exalted in the thought, a new one intruded. She was his. Now and forever there would never be another man who would own her soul, her body, her heart the way this man did.

Her heart hammered in her chest. Her breath stopped in her lungs. She sighed unsteadily.

"Clif."

His mouth covered hers, stifling her cry, and the pleasure built once more, until she thought she would die from it. Passion shuddered through her, wave after wave of it, completely overpowering her.

Afterward, they lay locked together, their breathing shallow, lips touching, as the wind sighed and whispered against the windows. Inside the chalet, the fire burned down to embers, and the wedding dinner grew cold. And two hearts slowly settled into a steady rhythm, as husband and wife continued to hold each other in an intimate embrace.

Chapter Twelve

I wish we didn't have to leave."

Alexandra settled herself comfortably in the limousine that would take them to the airport.

"If there weren't so many problems at the company right now, we'd stay on." Clif brushed his lips tenderly over hers, then pulled her close. "But I promise you we'll have a real honeymoon soon."

"It couldn't get any better than this."

He gave her a smile and dropped his arm around her shoulders.

As the car sped away, she turned for a last glimpse of the chalet where they had spent two glorious days and nights. They'd walked along snow-covered trails unsullied by other footprints, feeling as if they were the only two people in the world. They had sipped wine in front of a roaring fire and talked long into the night, exchanging long-held secrets. And they had made love with a passion, with a tenderness that staggered them and left them hungry for more.

Alexandra had never dreamed love could be so fulfilling. With Clif she felt complete. Never again would she feel lonely. Never again would she look back, only forward toward a bright, happy future.

They had taken a horse-drawn sleigh into town, where Alexandra shopped for Milly and Charley. Her hand moved to the small diamond heart at her throat. Clif had taken her into a jeweler's and surprised her with it. When she'd protested that it was far too expensive, he had silenced her objection by stating that this was just the first of many gifts he intended to lavish on her.

"After our managerial meeting I'd like to take you and Charley away for the holidays."

"Sounds heavenly."

He glanced down at her head, snuggled against his broad shoulder. Touching a tiny frown line between her eyes, he whispered, "Something's on your mind, Alex. What is it?"

The question startled her. She snuggled closer against him, feeling a tremor of apprehension. "The managerial meeting."

"What about it?"

"There are some...unpleasant things I'll have to deal with before that meeting." She drew away a little to look up at him. "I haven't wanted to talk about my problems at work because I wanted to handle them myself. I was hoping to tell you when I got to the bottom of everything."

He went very still. A muscle began to work in the side of his jaw. She saw the slight narrowing of his eyes. Then he relaxed and gave her a smile. "Why don't you try telling me now."

She took a deep breath. "Someone in Division Two is leaking our test results to the press, often before they're even revealed to the rest of the company." She chanced a quick glance at his face. Seeing no emotion, she plunged on. "I've been looking into it quietly. Most of the evidence points to someone very close to me." Her voice lowered. "For a few weak moments, I actually suspected my assistant, Mike Miller."

"What changed your mind?"

"Nothing I can put my finger on, I suppose. Call it intuition. I trust Mike completely."

As he expelled his breath angrily, she added quickly, "Mike isn't capable of such a vicious act, Clif."

"Why?" Reaching into his breast pocket, Clif shook a cigarette from his pack and held a gold lighter to the tip. He was jealous, he thought with surprise. Jealous of the young man who had her loyalty. It was an alien feeling, and Clif had to fight to put it aside, to remain objective.

"Call it an instinct." She shrugged. "Mike's been my assistant for two years now. I trust him."

His tone was sharper than he'd intended. "If it isn't Mike Miller, who could it be?"

She stared down at her hands. "Someone who's found a way to get the test results as soon as they're known, and someone who, for reasons unknown to me, wants to hurt the company."

Clif's voice was commanding. "A name, Alex. I need a name."

She looked up then and met his cool eyes. "Bill Campbell."

He stiffened. One of his aunt's favorite employees. His tone hardened. "Bill's been with the company for years. Why should he suddenly turn against us? And," he added sharply, "how is it that someone so recently promoted should be his accuser?"

She licked her lips. "I don't have all the proof yet. Just a feeling." She told him about the locked file and the key on the floor and her belief that papers in her briefcase had been rearranged. "Before I left, I went through my private file. The pages were out of order. I think if I were to go to his home I'd find photocopies of all the test results that have been compiled in our division in the past few months."

Beside her, Clif had grown very quiet. Bill Campbell had been in line for Alexandra's job. She might be unaware of that fact, but Bill had known that he was being considered. And someone had gone to a lot of trouble to make Alexandra look guilty. Clif remembered the investigator's two Gs. Greed and grudge. It all fit.

Unfortunately, his aunt would consider this another slap in the face. He'd have to walk a tightrope if he was going to avoid an explosion within the board.

Mistaking his silence, she touched his arm. "I shouldn't have bothered you with all this until I had more proof."

He stubbed out the cigarette and drew her close again. "I wish you'd told me sooner. You're so damned independent. But I'm glad you were finally able to confide in me." So glad that he felt relief shudder through him as he pressed his lips to her hair. Keeping his tone casual, he said, "I've been thinking that you might like to take a leave of absence, now that we're married. It would give you more time to be with Charley."

His comment took her by surprise. Was he hoping to put some distance between her and the accused? Or was there more? Was he uncomfortable about having his wife in the company? "It's been so long since I haven't needed to work; I probably wouldn't know what to do all day." She chuckled. "But it's tempting."

He touched her cheek. "I want whatever will make you happy, Alex."

It was an odd feeling, she realized, to be pampered. Though she considered herself an independent woman, she had a yearning to be taken care of. What in the world was happening to her?

The limousine drew up at the airport. As the driver loaded their luggage aboard the company jet, Clif helped Alexandra on board. "I'll be back in a minute. I have to make a phone call."

Almost as soon as he returned, they were airborne. Seated side by side on high-backed recliners, they clasped hands and sipped chilled wine.

"Martha will be delighted with the news of our wedding," Clif said with a smile. "I'm sure she'll want to plan some sort of reception for the employees."

Alexandra felt her heart tumble. "Reception. Oh, Clif," she breathed. He felt her hand tighten in his. "I don't know if I could handle something so public."

"You'd better get used to it." He laughed. "There will be a lot of curiosity about the new Mrs. Andrews."

Flashbulbs. Reporters. Gossip. Her family. Charley. Fear showed in her eyes.

"Clif, I'll need some time."

Glancing over, he lifted her hand to his lips. "I'd give you anything you asked for, Alex. But time..."

"Please." Her fear was becoming panic.

Reluctantly he nodded. "But don't make me wait too long." Pointing to a deeply-cushioned sofa along one wall, he said, "Why don't you rest. It's going to be a long flight."

She accepted his offer gratefully and sank down among the cushions. He covered her with a mohair throw and brushed his lips over her temple, feeling the rush of heat he always felt at touching her. It would be wonderful to lie beside her, to make love with her as they crossed the darkened sky. But she looked so exhausted, so vulnerable. Maybe the emotions of the weekend were catching up with her. He forced himself to walk away. To keep his mind occupied, he opened his briefcase and lifted out a folder.

Alexandra sensed that a barrier had been erected between them. He was so silent, so pensive. Was he already regretting his impulsive actions? The closer they came to home, the harder it would be to hold on to the dream.

Her lids fluttered. Weariness overpowered her. Unable to fight it, she dozed. In her dreams, Clif's face blurred to that of another, and he was backing away into the mist, until he had completely disappeared, leaving her alone and frightened.

When she awoke, she felt completely disoriented.

"How long have I been asleep?"

Clif looked up from his papers. "Better than two hours."

"I'm sorry. I haven't been much company."

"It doesn't matter. I have a lot of paperwork that won't wait. Would you like something to eat or drink?"

She shook her head.

"You don't mind if I take care of this?" He indicated the folders in his hand.

"No." She swung her feet to the floor and sat up. Her limbs still felt heavy with sleep. "I'll find something to read."

While they flew over snowcapped mountains and the lights of cities winking far below in the darkness, Clif buried himself in his work. Each time Alexandra glanced over at him, she reminded herself of the tremendous responsibility he carried. Still, she couldn't help feeling a twinge of sadness. After two glorious days of loving attention, was the honeymoon over? Was he regretting his impetuous act? What would his aunt say? His friends and employees? Everything between them seemed to be changing, and she sensed that it had all begun to unravel when she'd mentioned her suspicions about Bill Campbell.

It was nearly midnight when Clif drove her to her door.

"I wish you could stay the night at my house," he muttered, carrying her luggage up the front steps.

"It's too late to wake Charley." She held the front door, then led him to the living room, where a single light burned.

Milly was asleep on the sofa, with an afghan tucked warmly around her.

Seeing her, Alexandra turned to Clif. "I won't wake her. She may as well spend the night right there."

Clif deposited her suitcases, then walked back to the door. Putting a finger on his lips to silence him, Alexandra raised her face for a last kiss.

"It's only for a night," she said, before he could voice his protest once more. "Tomorrow, over dinner, we can break the news to Charley together."

He gathered her close and covered her mouth with his. His hand roamed her body possessively.

"One night," he growled, "and then I don't ever want us to be apart again."

She felt the urgency in his kiss, and her body responded. If it took forever, she would make him glad he'd married her. Weakly she clutched his waist for support.

"Take the morning off, Alex," he whispered. "You need time to unpack."

She felt a tingle of fear. Did he hope to keep her away from the office? "I can't just skip work."

"That's an order from the company president. Understand?"

A slow smile spread across her face. "Good night, Mr. Andrews," she murmured.

"Good night, Mrs. Andrews." With a last lingering kiss, he turned and walked to his car.

"Where've you been? You missed all the excitement." Mike Miller came running the moment Alexandra entered the office.

"What excitement?" As she dropped her briefcase on her desk top, she noted the time. Twelve o'clock. Clif hadn't said anything about taking the afternoon off.

"Bill Campbell has been accused of leaking test results to competitors and to the media."

Alexandra slumped down in her chair. "When?"

Mike shrugged. "I'm not sure. There are a dozen different rumors going through the company. Apparently he was visited late last night by a private investigator. When he didn't show up this morning, his secretary called and was told he wouldn't be returning to the company. The rest is mostly speculation." He looked elated. "Didn't I tell you there was something wrong with that guy?"

Dazed, Alexandra could only nod her head. "Who hired the private investigator?"

He lifted an eyebrow. "Don't know that, either. Probably the company. Maybe the board of directors know more than we give them credit for."

It was all happening so quickly. Her mind couldn't seem to grasp everything. "You don't know any more than that, Mike?"

"As soon as I hear anything, you'll be the first to know."

She gave him a weak smile as he swung through the doorway. The moment she was alone, she dialed Clif's number. His secretary informed her that Mr. Andrews would be in conference the rest of the afternoon.

* * *

Martha looked up from her desk as Clif's aunt strode past. "I'm sorry, Mr. Andrews isn't in his office just now."

"I know. I'll wait." Without another word, Marion opened the door and closed it firmly behind her. She had left the board meeting while Clif was still accepting accolades from the others. As always, he had come out of this looking like a white knight.

Taking the leather seat behind his desk, she spread her hands on the smooth top and glanced around the luxuriously appointed office.

It should have been hers, she thought angrily. Her father had never bothered to notice that she was better qualified to run the company than her younger brother. After Clif's father took over the reins of the company, all he really cared about was that silly football team. He was like a child with his toys. And now his son resembled him in a lot of ways. Too easygoing. Never willing to go for the jugular in a fight. His so-called scruples always got in his way.

So the leaks were stopped for now. Until, she thought angrily, the next disgruntled employee decides to take revenge because of some real or imagined slight. She would have fired them, one at a time, until the guilty party was found. In an atmosphere of fear, employees would be willing to give a lot more. Too much deadwood, she thought, tapping one manicured nail on the desk top. But Clif was too sentimental to get rid of them. Take Emmet. The old man was an embarrassment to the company. Always running those paint and chemical tests, always looking for the perfect automobile finish. She shook her head in annoyance. There was no such thing as a paint impervious to road salt and weather. The man was a fool.

The phone rang, shattering her thoughts. Picking it up, she said absently, "Yes?"

A bored female voice asked, "Mr. Clif Andrews's office?"

"Yes. Mr. Andrews is out."

Before she could hang up, she heard, "This is the Little Chapel of the Sierras. We have a tape available of the ceremony between Mr. Andrews and his bride, plus several photographs that we think will make lovely mementos of the occasion. Would Mr. and Mrs. Andrews like them mailed?"

Marion's mouth dropped open in shock. Her voice came out in a squeak. "The bride." She swallowed and took a deep breath. "The bride's name is . . . ?"

"Alexandra Porter Andrews."

Her mouth went dry. Her eyes narrowed. Of course. The sly Miss Porter.

"Do you think they would be interested in buying the tape and pictures?"

Marion's voice was steadier now. The shock hadn't worn off, but she was back in control. "I seriously doubt it. They've probably already had time to come to their senses and regret their foolish action. Just file those . . . mementos in the nearest wastebasket."

Hearing the little gasp on the other end of the line, Marion replaced the receiver and sat silently, drumming her fingers on the desk top. Her fool of a nephew had married that ambitious little tramp. If he couldn't see how such a marriage was going to ruin his future, she'd have to take matters into her own hands. It still wasn't too late.

Alexandra set the steaks in a marinade as Milly had shown her. She insisted on making this dinner by herself. She had left word with Clif's secretary that she would expect him by seven o'clock. Her plan was that she and Clif would tell Charley about their marriage, then after dinner the three of them would go over to Milly's house and share their happy news with her.

Charley was at Milly's house right now, practicing her ballet. It was to be their last time together. The three of them had already had a tea party to celebrate Milly's departure for Chicago in the morning. This time she was leaving for good. They had shed buckets of tears, and Alexandra's emotions were still very close to the surface.

When the doorbell rang, Alexandra looked up impatiently. She wanted this dinner to be perfect. She didn't need any interruptions. She was already nervous enough. Wiping her hands on a towel, she hurried to the front door.

At the unexpected sight of Clif's aunt, Alexandra was speechless.

"May I come in?"

She stood aside. Marion surveyed the room with a critical glance, then chose a straight high-backed chair. Her glossy ermine coat swirled about her ankles as she sat down.

"It must be a relief for you to know that Bill Campbell has been accused of leaking test results," Marion said without preamble.

"A relief?" Alexandra sat on the edge of the sofa, the kitchen towel still dangling from her hands. "I'm glad the leaks have been stopped. But I'm sorry for him. I'd hoped I was wrong about him."

Marion gave her a bright smile and leaned forward conspiratorially. "Well, I know it's a relief for my nephew. He was so afraid you were the guilty party."

"Me?"

Seeing Alexandra's color fade suddenly, Marion said sweetly, "You can imagine how it would look if Clif Andrews's 'good friend' should turn out to be using him. I'm sure the board would demand his resignation. Especially since his position is tenuous, at best." She lowered her voice conspiratorially. "I'm sure Clif considered confronting you with his suspicions. But what if you were to deny everything?" She shrugged her shoulders slightly. "He needed to get close enough to you to have your confidence."

Alexandra felt disgust rising like bile in her throat. Close enough. Was being married close enough? Clif had ordered an investigator to Bill Campbell's house even before they'd left Lake Tahoe. Too late, she remembered his phone call from the airport. And afterward, he'd become vague and withdrawn. Her voice was barely more than a whisper. "And what if I'd turned out to be the guilty party?"

"With a man like Clif, one never knows. I told him he couldn't take on the problems of the entire world. But you know Clif." Marion gave a little sigh. "He took in that ugly little pup because it needed a home. He's like that, always taking in strays. He probably worried that you'd lose your job. It wouldn't be easy, of course, to find a position with another auto company in this town with so many shadows on your reputation."

Alexandra's eyes narrowed. "What do you mean, 'so many shadows' on my reputation?"

Marion hoped she looked properly embarrassed. "I meant your child, of course. This is, after all, a small community. There can't be too many people who don't know about you, and about your family."

Alexandra's face was deathly white. "How long have you known about me?"

"From the first time I saw you. I knew your grandmother. I remember the pain she caused her daughters when she foolishly ran off with her chauffeur." Marion's voice lowered. "And I remember how your poor mother and father fled town rather than face a second scandal in their family."

She stood, pulling on her leather gloves. "Now that your job is secure, Miss Porter, you won't have to continue your 'intimate' friendship with my nephew. Unless, of course, you've decided that job security isn't enough." She gave a mirthless laugh. "Maybe you'd like to get your hands on the Andrews fortune, as well. But I warn you, I won't stand by and watch my family dragged to the level of yours. Clif thinks he's done something noble by rescuing you before your reputation could be further damaged." Her voice lowered ominously. "But you and I know better, don't we?"

Seeing the stricken look on Alexandra's face, she swept past her. "Don't bother seeing me to the door. I can find my way out."

Alexandra's mind reeled. Clif had suspected her of those leaks. And he'd needed to get close enough to know the truth. Close enough to push her into a hurried marriage? Was Marion right? Had he pitied her? Was that the reason? Obviously, the board couldn't demand the resignation of his wife. When the pressure was off, a marriage, especially one as impetuous as theirs, could easily be annulled. She felt faint. It was all happening again. The joy, the love, the euphoria had turned into pain, betrayal. When was she ever going to learn? When would she stop trusting soft words, sweet lies?

Long after the door closed behind her, Alexandra continued to sit numbly on the sofa, staring at the spots of bright color on the towel clutched in her hands.

"Milly, would you give this letter to Clif, please?"

The housekeeper took one look at Alexandra's pale features and caught her hand. "My Lord. You look like death. Are you coming down with something?"

"Milly." Alexandra pressed the letter into her friend's hand and lifted red-rimmed eyes to hers. "Please don't ask any questions. I'm taking Charley away for the holidays."

"Away? The last I heard you were making dinner for Clif Andrews."

"Everything's changed." Wiping away a tear, Alexandra said, "I have some tough decisions to make. Charley and I need to be alone."

"I'll help you pack."

"It's done. The bags are in the car." Turning, she said calmly, "Get your parka on, honey. We're leaving."

Bewildered, the little girl slid her feet into warm boots and pulled on her ski jacket. Alexandra hugged the older woman.

"Whatever has gone wrong, you ought to stay and face it, Alexandra," the older woman said softly. "Running away never solved anything." She placed a work-worn hand on either side of Alexandra's face and studied her. "I know this is an emotional time for you, what with my leaving and your problems at work and—" she pursed her lips "—whatever is between you and Clif."

"Oh, Milly, I'll miss you so, but I have to do this." She choked back a sob. "I'll never forget you, or all the loving things you did for Charley and me. If it weren't for you..."

"Nonsense," Milly said, bending down to hug Charley. "You two will manage just fine." She stood and placed her hand on the young woman's shoulder. "You're a strong woman, Alexandra Porter. Stronger than you think."

As the car pulled away from the curb, the big woman stood in the light of the entrance foyer, watching their departure through a blur of tears.

They drove for hours into the gathering darkness of the Northern Michigan night. Following a faded map, Alexandra found the snug cottage nestled among tall pines. A dirt road ran from the highway through the woods to the front door.

Charley had fallen asleep finally. The steady rhythm of the wheels had lulled her, despite her questions, tears and unhappiness. For the first two hours she had argued that the only thing she wanted for Christmas was to be at home with the tree she and Clif had decorated. Her words only added to her mother's heartbreak.

Bringing the car to a stop, Alexandra trudged through knee-high snow to the front door. Taking the key from its ancient case, she turned it in the lock and was relieved to feel the door open. Switching on the lights, she stared around at the ghostly furniture, draped in white covers.

Upstairs she uncovered the bed in the smaller bedroom. Memories came flooding back to Alexandra, memories of wonderful summers spent with her grandmother here at the lake. Looking around, she realized that this bedroom had been left exactly as she remembered it. Removing the covers from the rest of the furniture, she ran a hand lovingly over the old dresser top, complete with frilly dresser scarves and a mirrored tray covered with a collection of crystal miniatures. On a shelf was a photograph of Alexandra when she was nine, with her arm around her grandmother's waist. It had been taken one summer when her father and mother had traveled to Europe, leaving her in the care of the household staff. Her grandmother had rescued her and surprised her with a wonderful carefree summer idyll.

Hurrying downstairs, she carried her sleeping daughter inside and put her to bed. For the next hour, she uncovered the furniture in each room, shaking the dusty covers outside. When at last she had a fire blazing in the fireplace, she made herself a cup of tea and gave in to the overwhelming feelings of sadness.

Listless, she climbed the stairs to her grandmother's big bedroom. Sitting down on the big four-poster, she smiled, remembering the times she had sat beside her grandmother, drinking hot chocolate and giggling at her gentle teasing. How empty, she thought, her life would have been without Charlotte Van Allen.

Slowly undressing, she folded her clothes and opened a dresser drawer. Inside she found a faded photograph album. After pulling on a warm robe, she went downstairs and began leafing through the yellowed pages. The flames in the fireplace burned down to embers while she sat entranced, steeped in loving memories. Between the last page and the cover of the album, Alexandra found an envelope with her name on it. For long moments, she stared in surprise. Slowly she withdrew a sheet of lavender-tinted stationery. On it she read her grandmother's last letter to her, obviously written shortly before her death:

Dearest Alexandra,
I know that at this moment you are faced with some painful grown-up decisions. Right now, your future must surely appear bleak. I want you to cling to the belief that somewhere in this world you will find a man who will love you and your baby for yourselves—a man who will cherish you, who will care nothing for your name or your family history, but who will love you in a special way. With such a man you can share laughter, tears, love. With such a man you will know life's greatest treasure. Settle for nothing less.

All evening she had held the tears at bay. Now they flowed, streaming down her cheeks, dampening the collar of her robe. She cried for the child she had been and the child upstairs who trusted her. She cried for the man who had been all the things Gram had wished for her, and for the man who had used her for his own selfish purposes. She cried for all her dreams which would never come true now.

Clif drove like a madman. The letter Alexandra had written him lay crumpled on the seat beside him. He knew every painful word by heart. They were burned into his mind.

She'd written of his aunt's visit, of Marion's assertion that he'd married her in the hopes that she would let down her guard and tell him everything she knew about the security problem. She'd mentioned his weakness for strays, and insisted that she and Charley could take care of themselves. And finally she had promised to sign any annulment papers his lawyers drew up, assuring him that she would make no claim on his estate.

Milly couldn't tell Clif where Alexandra and Charley had gone. But he'd known. He'd seen the light in Alexandra's eyes when she spoke of her grandmother's cottage. Where else would she go to hide from the world?

The snow had been falling since he'd left home. Here in the north, the world was silent, frozen. Straining in the darkness, he saw the lights. Swinging off the highway, he followed the trail through the woods and pulled up behind her snow-covered car.

Alexandra's head jerked up at the knock on the door. There was no one around for miles, and no one knew she was here. She'd made certain of that.

Going to the door, she pulled the dusty curtain aside and stared at the figure standing on the porch. She pulled open the door and stood in the doorway, barring his entrance.

"How did you find me?"

He heard the anger in her voice but ignored it, clinging instead to the look that had come into her eyes in that first unguarded instant when she'd seen him. There was hope, he told himself, if he was careful.

"I remembered how much you said you loved your grandmother's cottage."

A gust of wind caused her to shiver, and he pressed his shoulder against the heavy wooden door to close it. When he turned, she fled across the room, standing in front of the fireplace.

Her hair was the color of flame, and he wanted to touch it, to plunge his hands into that thick tangle of curls. Instead he put his hands into his pockets in a careless pose and took a few steps closer.

"I read your letter, Alex."

"And you brought the annulment papers?"

His eyes narrowed. This wasn't going to be easy. "I want to talk about what my aunt told you."

"I suppose I should consider myself lucky," she said interrupting him. "At least one member of the family had the decency to tell me the truth."

"There wasn't time. Everything happened so fast." He began to walk closer. "I guess I've just fallen into the habit of doing things my way, without explanation."

"Not this time, Clif."

He heard the ice in her voice and froze. Now that he was closer he could see the blue smudges beneath her eyes. She looked tired. And she'd been crying. For him? His heart lurched. He hated himself for letting her get hurt by all this.

"You thought I was the one leaking those test results." Her words were spoken softly.

"You were a suspect, along with everyone in Division Two. But I never believed you were guilty."

"But I was a suspect even before you began seeing me. That was why you came to my house that first time. To see if you could trick me."

His voice lowered. "Don't, Alex. That isn't true. I came to see you because I was intrigued. And before I knew it, I was hooked. You were like a drug. I couldn't stop seeing you."

"You wanted to break down my resistance, to find out all I knew. When you couldn't get me into your bed any other way, you resorted to marriage."

"You can't believe that."

"Liar! You tricked me. You cheated. I trusted you, Clif. And you betrayed that trust."

Her eyes were dry, her spine straight. He knew that look. She wouldn't be defeated. This was the way he loved her. This was what he admired about the proper Alexandra Porter.

"I used every trick in the book to get you to marry me quickly, before you could think of a good reason not to," he said in a low, grating voice. He took a step closer and reached out a hand to her hair.

Heat raced along her spine. She felt her knees grow weak at his touch.

"I won't be made to feel guilty about that. I love you, Alex. I'm obsessed with you. And if it takes me the rest of my life, I'll prove to you how desperately I love you."

"And your aunt? How do you explain the things she said and did?"

His voice was toneless. "I have no control over Marion."

"But she knew all about me. Are you saying you two never discussed my past?"

"We never discussed your past or your future," he said. "I make it my business to live my life independent of what others think. I'd advise you to do the same." He tugged on her hair, forcing her head up. "Look at me, damn it. I could never betray you. I'd rather cut out my heart."

Alexandra examined the pain in his eyes. How had she ever thought him cold, unfeeling? He was the only man who had ever touched her heart in this special way. Trust? When she was this close, she knew instinctively that she could trust him. And despite the doubts his aunt had planted in her mind, she knew in her heart that he was too honorable to lie about something this important.

But she'd trusted before, and that trust had been betrayed. Why did she believe Clif was different? Because, her heart whispered, Clif Andrews was an honorable man. A man worthy of trust. She stared at him as if her vision had cleared suddenly.

"I think it's time I stopped living in the past," she said simply.

His heart seemed to stop beating.

Slowly, gradually, humor flashed in her eyes. "So I take it an annulment is out of the question."

His eyes narrowed. Now what was she up to? "Absolutely."

She wrapped her arms around his neck and brought her lips to within inches of his. "Then I believe you owe me another honeymoon. The first was too short."

He bent his head, but she pulled away, taunting him with the nearness of her lips. "And you did say something about taking Charley and me away for the holidays."

His gaze focused on her mouth, and he pulled her close. When he found her lips, they both felt the heat blaze between them.

"There's a big old bed that used to be my grandmother's," she whispered against his lips, causing him to moan and crush her to him. As the kiss deepened, she felt her pulse race. It would always be like this when he touched her. "I suggest we start that honeymoon tonight. And first thing in the morning, after we share our secret with Charley, you two can go out in the woods and cut another tree."

He ran his hand lightly along her back and felt her tremble at his touch. "I like the way you think, lady," he muttered against her lips.

He banked the need to take her here on the bare wood floor of the cottage. Reaching into his pocket, he withdrew a small silver box. Inside, nestled in velvet, was a simple gold band. He heard her little murmur of surprise as he placed it on her finger. "I can't have my wife going around in an oversize class ring." He kissed her finger, as if to seal the bargain. "There's no turning back, Alex. We're tied to each other. I'm going to love you forever."

"Forever." As he brought his lips to the hollow of her throat, she sighed. "I'm not sure that's going to be long enough."

"Then let's get started." He lifted her in his arms and climbed the stairs.

"Welcome home, Mr. Andrews."

There was a light in his eyes she'd never seen before. It said more than any words. "I love you, Mrs. Andrews."

COMING NEXT MONTH

LOGAN'S WOMAN—Glenda Sands
Susan belonged to another man—or so Clark Haggerty thought. And
it was up to Susan to reinforce that belief. But that was easier said
than done once she found herself falling in love with him.

TOMORROW'S DAWN—Frances Lloyd
Justine Carroll had once loved Marcus Glendinning, but he had
married another woman. Now he had returned, determined to win her
back. Did he deserve another chance?

LADY AND THE LEGEND—Sharon De Vita
Victoria Fairchild was a lady—even though she wasn't acting like one.
It couldn't have anything to do with Gator McCallister—could it?

BENEATH A SUMMER MOON—Juli Greene
Raising two sons and running a garden center kept widow
Janice Haley busy, but she longed for a man to make her feel like a woman
again. Why did that man have to be the impossible David Phillips?

KISSING GAMES—Pamela Toth
Supernerd or Superman? When Patricia MacGregor first saw
Brad McKinney, she almost died. This was her dream date? Oh, no!
Then Brad set out to remind her that Clark Kent was only a
disguise—what was underneath was the real thing.

STRANGE ENCHANTMENT—Annette Broadrick
One enchanted evening, teacher Elizabeth Bannister saw ad executive
Dan Morgan across a crowded room. Mesmerized, both of them
knew that their lives would never be the same again.

AVAILABLE THIS MONTH:

SATIN AND WHITE LACE
Barbara Turner

DARE TO DREAM
Cara Colter

THE PROPER MISS PORTER
Ruth Langan

PURSUED BY LOVE
Caty Lear

SUGAR AND SPICE
Debbie Macomber

THE PRIVATE GARDEN
Arlene James

You won't want to miss a single one of the heart-felt stories presented by Silhouette Special Edition; and when you take advantage of this special offer, you won't have to.

You'll also receive a FREE subscription to the Silhouette Books Newsletter as long as you remain a member. Each lively issue is filled with news on upcoming titles, interviews with your favorite authors, even their favorite recipes.

To become a home subscriber and receive your first 4 books FREE, fill out and mail the coupon today!

Silhouette Special Edition®

Silhouette Books, 120 Brighton Rd., P.O. Box 5084, Clifton, NJ 07015-5084

FOUR UNIQUE SERIES FOR EVERY WOMAN YOU ARE...

Silhouette Romance

Heartwarming romances that will make you laugh and cry as they bring you all the wonder and magic of falling in love.

6 titles per month

Silhouette Special Edition

Expanded romances written with emotion and heightened romantic tension to ensure powerful stories. A rare blend of passion and dramatic realism.

6 titles per month

Silhouette Desire

Believable, sensuous, compelling—and above all, romantic—these stories deliver the promise of love, the guarantee of satisfaction.

6 titles per month

Silhouette Intimate Moments

Love stories that entice; longer, more sensuous romances filled with adventure, suspense, glamour and melodrama.

4 titles per month

Silhouette Romances
not available in retail outlets in Canada

SIL-GEN-1A